A Song For Lisa

Clifton LaBree

Published by
Fading Shadows Imprint
New Boston, New Hampshire

Paperback ISBN: 978-0-9746450-7-0

Cover by Vivian LaBree
Back Ground Photo By Michael LaBree

A story of courage that is a tribute to the human spirit. This novel is fictional, but descriptions of the Japanese treatment of prisoners' of war during World War II is factual. The courage and resourcefulness of the US army's Rangers is typical of their daring exploits throughout the war.

Dedicated to my wife Pauline, and my family, with thanks for all their support and encouragement.

Chapter One

SECRET

FROM: Sixth Army Headquarters, Hollandia, New Guinea.

TO: First Lieutenant Jonathon Wright, Commanding Officer Ranger Platoon, Code-Name *Snapdragon*.

SUBJECT: Urgent change of orders.

New intelligence has arrived at this command making it imperative that your previous orders be canceled. Repeat, previous orders are canceled. Your new orders are as follows:

1. Maintain code name *Snapdragon*.
2. The USS Submarine *Tigerfish*, on which you and your thirty-five men are now embarked, will insert you on the northeastern coast of Lingayen Gulf at a point given to Captain Turner.
3. Your assault platoon of Rangers will be met by a Filipino guerrilla patrol at 2100 Hours on the evening of January 5, 1945.
4. You are ordered to link up with the Filipino patrol and advance inland approximately ten miles under the cover of darkness to a prison compound located at an old sugar cane plantation south of Baguio. Urgent intelligence indicates that the inmates, and women and children are in grave danger of being massacred!
5. The assault on Luzon is planned for 0600 Hours on January 9, 1945. It is imperative that you secure the prison compound and move the prisoners back along

the same route so that the submarine can pick them up prior to the assault on Luzon.

6. Memorize this message and burn in the presence of Captain of USS *Tigerfish*.

Lieutenant General Walter Kreuger

Commanding General Sixth Army.

Lieutenant Jonathon Wright read the message twice before handing it back to the tall, slender captain of the USS *Tigerfish*. "What do you make of it, Captain?" he asked, concerned that the well-rehearsed mission he and his men had been preparing for was canceled at the last minute.

"A number of long-range penetration missions in the Philippine Islands have been assigned to your Rangers," said Captain Turner. "The intelligence gathering services of MacArthur's Far East command has been efficient and reliable. My orders were changed at the same time. I have new coordinates for the point of land where you'll pick up the Filipino patrol. Your radioman can make contact with the sub at any time between 2100 and 2400 hours when we'll be running on the surface charging our batteries. If you get no answer from us it's because we're in danger of being discovered. Be patient and give us a little time to relocate before surfacing."

"I understand that, sir," answered the studious Ranger officer, still uncomfortable with the change in orders. "If the prisoners are sickly and weak, which is a very likely situation, how will we be able to transport them back to the coast?"

Captain Turner answered with a shrug of his shoulders. "Some of the partisans might be able to provide water buffalo carts for those unable to walk. We're at the end of the command chain, Lieutenant. I'm sure Sixth Army had just cause to alter your mission. They have more information than we do."

"The thing I like the least about this change is that success hinges on the performance of someone who's a stranger to us," Jonathon said, removing his Zippo lighter from his shirt pocket to burn the crumpled message in an ash tray on the wardroom table.

"You have a few hours to review this with your men, Lieutenant," announced Captain Turner, checking his watch. "We're on course to the rendezvous point for your contact with the partisans. We'll have you ashore shortly after 2100 hours. There'll be a full moon tonight."

"That suits me fine. The risk of discovery is greater with the added light, but we can travel faster and easier in unknown territory. I'll prepare the men. Thanks for everything, Captain Turner. I'm going to miss this cozy wardroom and your excellent coffee," he smiled.

"I wish you and your Rangers the best of luck, Lieutenant. You're making us all proud. The kind of humanitarian mission ahead of you separates the United States Army from the armies of the rest of the world. We'll be waiting for your return with open arms and a full complement of fresh brewed coffee!"

Lieutenant Jonathon Wright finished his coffee and left the wardroom. He was of medium height and build with sandy hair that always seemed uncombed. His expressive brown eyes could register sorrow and happiness in a single blink. He was a quiet studious young man. Most people liked him, yet he frequently kept to himself and selected his friends with care. Even though he was not as heavy or strong as many of the men in his command, there was an inner strength and conviction that made people feel at ease with him. He did not command his platoon, he led it by example with deep appreciation and consideration for the welfare of the men. They were inspired by his calm demeanor and would follow him anywhere. He had won their respect and affection which was a difficult juggling act for an officer to do. He never asked the men to do anything he would not do himself. His

3

willingness to go to bat for them when he felt they were not getting fair treatment always placed him on the side of the angels. Most who knew Jonathon would describe him as a stable and dependable young man who did what he said he would do without fanfare.

Jonathon was a graduate of the University of New Hampshire where he took advantage of the Reserve Officer Training Corps program to help pay his way through college. He had married his high school sweetheart from Monson, Maine, half way through college in 1939. Upon graduation with a degree in criminology June of 1941, he was offered a second lieutenant commission in the army. A full-time job as an officer had much appeal to him, especially the weekly paycheck. He was twenty-two years old when the war started.

Jonathon crouched to get through the small passage doors of the submarine making his way to the compartment where his men and their equipment were located. They were packed into the confined quarters of the submarine in and around the deadly gray torpedoes. He was worried. There were too many unknowns beyond his ability to control. How many Japanese were guarding the prison compound? How many prisoners were at the compound? What was their physical condition? A large body of people had more of a chance to be discovered by the Japanese. The Rangers were a lightly armed infantry unit with limited means of maintaining prolonged contact with the enemy.

Jonathon was assured that the maps of the area he possessed were detailed and accurate. It was relatively flat land near the coastal plain which made travel easy. A few miles inland the terrain undulated with streams, swamps and jungle that could eliminate the possibility of using native carts to transport to the coast those inmates unable to walk. Existing cart tracks and trails would be dangerous for them to use because the Japanese could control most of them. The prospect of leading a large ponderous train of liberated prisoners through enemy held territory sent shivers through Jonathon's body, but orders were meant to be obeyed.

Second Lieutenant Hal Jacobs, second in command of *Snapdragon*, was a tall muscular man with dark complexion and deep-set eyes. There was something ominous about him that grabbed a person's attention. His physical presence could be intimidating until he smiled, which was often. The grin brought out the easy going boyish nature in him that endeared him to the men. He never took himself seriously. A recent graduate of West Point Military Academy, he was anxious to do his part in winning the war. Jacobs had a pathological hatred for the Japanese. He read the look on Jonathon's face and expected to hear bad news.

"What's wrong, Jon?"

"Take a seat, Hal," suggested Jonathon, waving his arms for the men to gather around and listen. He spelled out the contents of their new orders. A low moan of disappointment filled the compartment. "I know what you're thinking, men. I had the same reaction, but it's a mission that we've been handed and we'll just have to make the best of it and carry it out. I want each of you to recheck your gear and mentally prepare yourselves for the task ahead of us. You've had the best training of any outfit in the United States combat services. I'm confident in your ability to adapt to any situation in which we find ourselves. Our original mission was to blow up strategic rail bridges to help isolate the beachhead. Now we won't need the demolition material. We can leave it behind on the submarine."

"Should we stock up on extra food rations, sir?" asked a voice from the top bunks.

"Smart thinking, soldier," replied Jonathon. "My thoughts are that we should make the initial drive inland loaded with extra ammo and grenades. Our radio man can contact our air coordinator for a drop of extra foodstuff if we need it. We also have the option of calling for close air support if it's absolutely necessary. I prefer remaining as elusive and invisible as possible until we get to the compound."

"What if carts aren't available to transport sick and injured prisoners?" asked a young soldier, sitting on the deck cleaning his M-1 Garand rifle. Jonathon looked at the young corporal and marveled at the youth of his command, which varied from seventeen to twenty-two. The average age was eighteen.

"I can't answer that, corporal. It's one of the unknowns we'll have to overcome as we go along. I assume that the Filipino partisans will be able to fill us in on matters like that. They'll also be able to describe the compound to us." Jonathon checked his watch and paused.

"Will we have time for chow before we leave the sub?" someone asked.

"Yes. The captain has assured me that the galley will stuff us full before we leave," Jonathon smiled. "If I had the room to carry it I'd bring along several thermos bottles of coffee, but so much for wishful thinking. Spend the rest of your time preparing for the mission by resting. Write home if you want. Leave the letters in the mailroom bins in the wardrooms. Men, this will be our first combat mission together and I feel confident that it'll be a success. In the years to come you'll be able to tell your grandchildren how you helped to liberate the Philippine Islands. We'll be the vanguard of the army that General MacArthur promised would return. You'll have plenty of time to gear up so relax as much as you can. Any questions?"

"This is our first mission with you, sir," said a short stocky man from Maine. He put into words what each man was thinking. "I know that you'll be worrying about a lot of things. I just wanted to let you know that no matter how tough it gets out there, we're with you one hundred percent. When the Japs meet this platoon, they're taking on the first team and they'll soon find out why we call ourselves the best."

A resonant cry of approval echoed from stem to stern on the submarine. Jonathon left the torpedo room with a broad smile on his lips and a warm glow in his heart. He had successfully bonded with the men and he had no reservations about their ability to close with the enemy.

Two hours later, a loud voice sounded over the submarine's intercom system. "This is Captain Turner speaking. We are approaching the northwestern shore of Lingayen Gulf. We will be discharging the Army Rangers within the hour in our inflatable rafts. They are some of the first Americans to enter occupied Luzon Island. Their mission is to rescue American prisoners now held by the Japanese and to escort them back to the coast where we'll pick them up. They embark on a dangerous mission filled with unknowns and leave with our best wishes and fervent prayers for success.

"They've earned our admiration and respect. May the angels guide them back to the *Tigerfish*. Godspeed Rangers. We'll surface in ten minutes and proceed as close to the shore as the tide permits."

Jonathon and the men checked their weapons one last time. Their ammunition belts were filled to capacity. A grim silence filled the sub as the squad leaders checked each man. The platoon was composed of three squads of eleven men each. The single file they formed wound in and around all of the torpedo compartments.

When the submarine surfaced, interior lights were turned off and replaced with dim red lamps to make the craft as invisible from prying eyes as possible. Sailors scurried from the conning tower and pulled the rubber inflatable rafts from the hull's hatches. As soon as they were inflated, the sailors lined them up on the deck.

The Rangers received word to load the rafts and began passing packs up through the small openings of the hatches. It took a while for the men to adjust to the darkness. The full

7

moon was visible in the western sky making the evening surprisingly light after they got used to it. Lieutenants Jacobs and Jonathon checked each boat and whispered encouragement to the men. The two sailors in each boat would return to the submarine once they had delivered the Rangers on land. Jonathon signaled with a raised fist for the submarine to submerge enough for the boats to become buoyant. The heavily loaded inflatables slowly began their journey to the enemy shore as the submarine dove out of sight.

Each man was left alone with his fears and anxieties. Fear was not altogether a bad emotion. In life-threatening situations it brought each person to the highest degree possible of alertness. They wondered if the enemy was waiting for them as soon as they stepped foot on shore. The island had over a half million Japanese soldiers, well dug in to repel any invasion from the Americans. Experience had shown the invading Americans just how stubbornly the Japanese defended their occupied territory to the last man alive.

The first boat, with Jonathon on board, acted as guide to coordinate the rendezvous point with the partisan fighters. The coastal region was sparsely populated and intelligence experts did not indicate any large body of enemy troops in the vicinity. Over the past three years, Jonathon had fought through the central Pacific area and knew that one should not put too much faith in intelligence information. It had a tendency to be wrong, regardless of the source.

The closer they got to the shore the more worried Jonathon became over the lack of response from the partisans. Captain Turner had assured him that the navigator on the sub was one of the best. The azimuth Jonathon was following to the shore seemed logical and correct, but he was increasingly apprehensive. They were on course. Where were the guerrillas? The navy paddlers guided the rafts into a small cove between two large rock formations and allowed the rafts to ride onto a small sandy beach. The Rangers silently evacuated the rafts and ran across the beach toward the thick vegetation farther inland where they set up a perimeter defense.

Before leaving the submarine Jonathon had informed Captain Turner that he was going to proceed with the mission with or without the partisans. Most of the men were veterans of several operations involving intelligence gathering and mapping of enemy installations. Without local guerrilla assistance, Jonathon knew that the platoon was somewhat blind and vulnerable. Unintentionally running into a heavy concentration of enemy troops was a very real scenario that could blow their cover.

The Rangers waited at the transition line between the beach and the jungle for several minutes listening to the sounds from the night. The normal cacophony of the nocturnal creatures of the jungle filled the warm, salty air. Nothing seemed unusual and Jonathon breathed a sigh of relief. So far so good! He hunkered close to the ground and unfolded his map while a soldier placed a poncho over his head to shield the light from his small flashlight. He studied the contours of the area between the coast and the sugar plantation where the prisoners were located. Laying his compass on the map he oriented it with the compass and penciled in a thin line to the compound. He memorized the azimuth of the line and checked his watch again. They had about seven hours of darkness to cover nine miles to the prison camp.

Jonathon had studied the maps of the area and was confident that they could cover the distance to the compound by dawn when they would lay low to rest and observe the activities of the prison community. There were few roads in the area which suited him. He preferred making the trip through the jungle where chances of discovery were less likely.

Two flanking scouts were sent out about one hundred feet on each side of the main body along the proposed line of travel. Lieutenant Jacobs was assigned the job of securing the tail of the column while Jonathon took the point position with the radioman at his side. He stood up to check the surrounding darkness fingering the safety on his Thompson submachine. For the first hour, he felt confident guiding the platoon by keeping the moon on his left shoulder. Every half hour he would stop to check his azimuth and realign the relative position of the moon which was constantly changing.

The tight column of Rangers cleared the heavier ground vegetation and found themselves under the relatively open canopy of a coconut plantation of widely spaced trees. Three men in dark clothing suddenly blocked Jonathon's inland movement. He clicked the safety on his Thompson and dropped to his knees, prepared to defend himself.

"We've been expecting you *Snapdragon*," announced a deep voice in broken English.

"I'm relieved to make contact with you," answered Jonathon warily, his finger still on the trigger.

"Let us take a moment to review what is ahead of us," suggested the tallest of the shadowy men touching Jonathon on his shoulder. "Please sit so that we can study our maps. We are relatively safe from detection within this plantation. My father owns it. I'm Sergeant Hammer of the Filipino Scouts. I assume that you are Lieutenant Wright."

Jonathon breathed easier and kneeled beside the Filipino sergeant. "I was beginning to worry that we had missed you, Sergeant Hammer."

"I apologize that I did not direct you to us with a light, but the Japanese have been more active lately with their shore patrols. We made certain that you were not threatened by the patrols. I thought it would be better for you to get away from the beach before we made contact," explained Sergeant Hammer, laying a map on the ground exactly like the one Jonathon had folded in his pocket.

Sergeant Hammer outlined the original mission which was being taken over by other Filipino units. As a matter of fact it was his group of guerrilla fighters that had recommended the change in plans. He had fifteen men with him to supplement the army platoon for the assault on the compound. His map had been updated with a more accurate layout of the sugar plantation where the women were being held prisoner.

Approximately thirty Japanese naval infantrymen were guarding the rectangular compound, which consisted of a barn and a stable completely enclosed by a barbed wire fence with elevated platforms at the four corners. Two men and a machine gun were located on each platform day and night. There was also a large two-story house immediately beside the horse stable. The guards were housed in a lean-to attached to the house. Sergeant Hammer believed that the house was being used by the officers. They had counted three officers but there may be more.

"How long will it take us to get there, Sergeant?" asked Jonathon.

"If we don't have to detour for Japanese patrols, we can be there by three o'clock in the morning. I have a small band of local partisans watching the compound from a nearby hillside. Our immediate destination is that overview. As soon as the sun comes up you can observe the camp and plan your assault."

"How many inmates are in the prison?" Jonathon asked.

"Our best estimate is about seventy-five," replied Sergeant Hammer.

"Seventy-five?" exclaimed Jonathon. "I was led to believe that it would be a couple of dozen. We couldn't get that many on the boat even if we made it back before the invasion! Why did you recommend that this mission be substituted for our previous one?"

"The family of one of my men brings supplies and vegetables to the guard detachment. A short time ago the original Japanese army guards were replaced by a fanatical Japanese naval infantry unit. They are much more brutal and oppressive to the women inmates. The sick list and the death rate of the inmates has doubled since the change in guards. Something else has been taking place at an alarming rate," Sergeant Hammer explained.

"What are you trying to say?"

"The inmates, young and old, are being beaten and raped by members of the detachment. Every night we hear their cries and screams from our overview position."

"My God!" cried Jonathon. A few of the men heard what the Filipino scout had told Jonathon. The grim message circulated from man to man galvanizing them into an avenging fighting unit. Now they understood the urgency of their mission.

"There's something else, Lieutenant," added Sergeant Hammer in a strained voice. He stood up grasping his Springfield bolt action rifle firmly. "The day that the Japanese detachment is informed of the American invasion of Luzon, they will not hesitate to kill every one of the prisoners. They want no live witnesses to the bestial behavior of the naval infantry. Massacring prisoners, military as well as civilian, has been a trademark of the Japanese throughout the Islands."

"Lead the way, Sergeant Hammer," ordered Jonathon with a stern set to his jaw. "Let's get Operation *Snapdragon* underway!"

Chapter Two

Evening shadows descended on the small sugar cane plantation known as Los Tomas. A cool sea breeze swept the surrounding jungle vegetation depositing its moist cleansing aroma throughout the confines of the barn and nearby horse stable. Occasionally the fetid stench of the prison compound was displaced by the cool trade winds, but when the night air became still and the winds shifted their direction, the dry putrid smells from the open latrine pits were overpowering. Unwashed human bodies added another dimension to the offensive foulness that permeated the two structures where the women prisoners were detained. They spent each day in the field planting, cultivating, and harvesting sugar cane and sugar beets. They were allowed a small area for the production of vegetables, which never reached maturity before the starving inmates consumed every stem as soon as it sprouted from the rich soil. Fear and despair hung over the prison camp. Death was commonplace.

During the earlier months of the war the inmates were treated poorly, but a strong element of hope permeated the atmosphere. The Caucasian female prisoners were secretaries, office workers, nurses, domestic workers, nannies, and school teachers. Many were married to consulate and government officials and military officers. Immediately upon surrendering they were separated from the men.

That first year, they were treated relatively well by the Japanese commandant who followed the covenants of the Geneva Convention. Good judgment was used in handling the female prisoners on the assumption that they may be returned to the Allies in exchange for Japanese officials arrested in Washington and London at the beginning of the war. Red Cross packages were regularly distributed. The inmates ate as well as the compound guards. There was a chance that they would be repatriated, but efforts to accomplish an exchange were feeble and infrequent.

The Japanese guard replacement took place in late 1942 when conditions began to deteriorate. Food became scarce even though the prisoners had cultivated a large area for the production of vegetables. At first it was passionately attended and met with the approval of the guard detachment. As hunger became commonplace the garden patch became nothing but a bare piece of ground. Even weeds were eaten as soon as they took root in the black soil.

A portion of the barn was converted into an infirmary where the nurses did all they could to care for the sick and those injured by the sadistic guards. The women persevered in the barbarous atmosphere and were thankful that the camp commandant held a tight grip on the men under his command. Physical cruelty, starvation, and denial of adequate medical treatment was commonplace for the next two years. As bad as it was, it could have been worse. The inmates were not used as sex objects by the Japanese. A few of the women made suggestive overtures to some of the guards for special treatment. The guards were tempted by the offers but they never followed through. The commandant would have severely punished them. Each guard was mortally afraid of raising his wrath against themselves.

The single symptom of prolonged malnutrition and starvation most feared by the prisoners was blindness. Every woman was suffering to some degree from the dreaded condition. Loss of vision and the ability to distinguish images at a distance were symptoms that caused the most anxiety among the prison population. The nurses tried to reassure them that normal sight would be restored once they were back on normal diets.

Malaria, dysentery, acute dehydration, and pellagra were but a few of the malignancies that proved to be fatal. The inmates were gaunt and weary, and had given up any hope they once had of freedom or of outliving the subhuman conditions imposed upon them. Their arms and legs were like straws on scarecrows that farmers fashioned in their corn fields to keep away crows. Their drawn, grotesque facial features were stretched tight against their protruding bone structure. Few would recognize themselves if they looked in a mirror.

Lisa Carter slept on a bamboo mat in the corner of the stable. The delicate facial features she once had were lost in the horror-filled deeply set eyes. Her auburn hair was unkempt and filthy like the tattered dress she wore.

Lisa was a tireless and energetic worker in the fields. She kept to herself as much as possible, but when help was needed by her fellow prisoners she was among the first to respond to their needs. She had been a civil service worker in the consulate general office in Manila when the war began. The Japanese had captured the city before any of the civilian workers could escape.

Lisa was among the first prisoners to be rounded up within the city and deposited at the abandoned sugar plantation known as Los Tomas. Over her shoulder she still carried a small pocketbook filled with personal items and identification cards and some American currency. She was dressed in a light blouse, skirt and blazer when the Japanese arrested her.

That first year the Red Cross supplied the inmates with enough clothing so that they could change from the clothes they were wearing when captured into something more suitable. Once the Red Cross source of supplies was eliminated, their tan pants and shirts became tattered and torn. The Japanese claimed not to have any replacement clothing for them. The main source of foodstuffs, blankets, and clothing came to the inmates by way of the local Filipino population who, almost on a daily basis, threw supplies over the barbed wire enclosure. Soap, shoes, and feminine hygiene products became precious possessions to those who were first to catch the items. Several ugly fights developed among the inmates scrambling for the provisions. In time the inmates were able to administer the distribution of the precious booty in a fair and equitable system.

One of the most influential ladies in the prison was a woman in her early sixties who called herself "Madame June." It was obvious to all of the inmates that she came from a family of influence and authority. She voluntarily took it upon herself to organize the compound into small groups with assigned leaders. Beyond that no one asked questions, for it could have been dangerous for true identities to be known. The main purpose of such a structure was to instill some semblance of order so that the supplies thrown to them could be administered justly and those most in need could be cared for. It was the "buddy system" on a larger scale than one on one.

Madame June had wisely selected individuals throughout the barn and stable to act as representatives for the groups. That gave the inmates some cohesion and identity with the group, allowing them to function as a society instead of an uncontrollable mob. She spoke in a straightforward manner with a slight southern drawl. The jewelry she brought with her to the compound she exchanged with the commandant for medicines and personal hygiene supplies. She became a beloved member of the prison community.

Small of stature with white hair, Madame June emanated confidence and hope. She was primarily responsible for establishing a more structured community within their squalid confinement. Her voice was soft and she selected her words carefully so as to not be misunderstood. She was a born leader, never demanding or giving orders. Things got done when she suggested that this or that needed attention and should be taken care of. Most of the inmates were eager to carry out her wishes. She was responsible for helping to maintain their sanity and self-respect in the face of inhuman cruelty and complete indifference to their suffering.

One of Madame June's closest companions was the young woman known as Lisa. Many speculated that they had known each other before the war started, but neither gave any indication that that was the case. Pseudonyms were common and readily accepted by the incarcerated community. Here it did not make any difference who they had been. Each individual was accepted or rejected on the basis of who and what they were within the enclosed barbed wire fence. Within a short time after Madame June recognized the need for some discipline within the camp, the emotionally stronger women began to assume positions of leadership. It was a loose alliance that worked well.

Madame June worked tirelessly for the women, holding several in her arms through long difficult nights when they were ill or distraught, and in need of comfort.

Malaria was the most debilitating disease. The Japanese claimed that they did not have any quinine, a medicine that gave relief to patients suffering from the disease. One day late in June, 1942, Madame June demanded that she be taken to the prison commandant to whom she argued forcefully and defiantly for quinine and other medicines. She promised the commandant that she would produce gold jewelry in exchange. He insolently told her that he could take the gold if he wanted without producing the medical supplies. Everyone who heard the discussion remembered the words Madame June spoke in precise English which the commandant understood.

"You may kill me and torture me but I can promise that I will never tell you where the jewelry is hidden. You produce the medicine and I'll produce the payment. Take it or leave it. Don't misunderstand what I'm telling you, Mr. Commandant. You and your henchmen will never be able to break me. You might kill me, but I've already lived a full life and am prepared to die. The decision is yours."

The commandant was furious to be backed so neatly into a corner by an old lady weighing no more than one hundred and ten pounds. He carefully scrutinized Madame June and Lisa, who had accompanied her to the main plantation house. He was anything but stupid and believed that the elderly matron meant what she said. He curtly dismissed them. The next day the front gates were opened and two carts piled with boxes were wheeled into the compound. The soldiers asked for Madame June. She instructed the women to take the boxes to the small infirmary in a corner of the barn. The guards were reluctant to release the carts until Madame June and Lisa walked to the open gate behind the carts and motioned to the guards. She held a gold necklace and two gold rings in her hand offering them to the guards. Their demeanor immediately changed. They released the cart and grabbed the jewelry without a word. The gate was closed behind them in their haste to bring the fortune in gold to their superior. That had been a good period for the inmates. Madame June had won a moral victory.

During the second year of the women's internment, two B-26 bombers flew over the compound a few feet above the barn roof maintaining their position one behind the other. As they approached the fence enclosure their bomb bay doors began to discharge thousands of small packages from the cavernous fuselages. The boxes rained upon the compound and buildings covering the ground several layers thick in places. The pilot's aim was precise, most of their load fell within the prison complex. Loud cheers erupted from the inmates as they scrambled for the boxes and waved at the screaming planes overhead. As soon as the planes were empty, they made a turn and retraced their path over the compound again with their left wings tilted straight down so that the inmates could get a good look at the pilots, as they rocked their wings back and forth in salute.

It was a thrilling experience for every member of the prison. The presence of American bombers meant that American forces were approaching the Philippine Islands. That fact energized the lagging hopes and fears of being isolated from the rest of the world. Familiar American products also rekindled pride in who they were. The small packages sustained their belief in eventual deliverance from their unspeakable hell.

The packages were called "Victory Packs." They were wrapped in paper containing the American and Filipino flags and a line made famous by General Douglas MacArthur: "I Shall Return." They contained American cigarettes, Chesterfield, Lucky Strikes, Philip Morris, or Kools. The candy portion was either Hershey chocolate bars, Skybars, or Mounds, with generous amounts of Tootsie-Rolls, and chewing gum (Juicy-Fruit, Doublemint or Teaberry). The compact package also contained a pencil with a paper pad, and something that the women treasured — a small sewing kit with extra thread. The packages that fell outside of the fence were also eagerly sought by the Japanese guard detachment. They scrambled and fought for them the same as the inmates.

The Victory Packs were the brainchild of General MacArthur's Army staff. The idea came from his Intelligence chief, Major General Charles Willoughby. The packs helped keep the flame of liberty and hope alive. Their value as a morale booster was far greater than the cost of assembling small tokens from a free nation. They were a piece of Americana representing the might and will of a country and its people who had not forgotten the plight of the Filipinos. Packages that fell into the hands of the enemy were ominous reminders that their days of control in the Philippines were limited.

Lisa and Madame June had surrendered to the Japanese at the Manila Library. Madame June was in the reading room when the enemy soldiers surrounded the building and began collecting occupants as they went from room to room. Lisa was in the archival portion of the library researching records of past census surveys. The Japanese immediately dismissed all of the native Filipinos and retained the Americans and other nationalities for incarceration in holding camps located throughout the occupied area of the islands.

The civilian males were separated from the children and women at the train station in Manila. The men were considered the same as military prisoners of war and were marched off to prisons in the city proper. The women and older children were loaded on empty freight cars which transported them a hundred and fifty miles north of Manila near the small town of Bagio. They were then forced to walk five miles over sugar cane fields to a deserted plantation where Japanese soldiers were diligently building a wire fence around the outbuildings of the plantation. The women were told that they were temporarily being detained until reparation could be arranged through the International Red Cross and the offices of neutral countries such as Switzerland and Sweden. The Japanese commandant spoke excellent English and even apologized for the primitive living conditions at the camp. At the time of Lisa and Madame June's arrival, there were about fifty women and teen-aged children already being held captive at the plantation.

Life at the camp was difficult for the first year but most of the inmates were able to maintain their physical and emotional sense of well-being without any threat or fear of the type of sadistic abuse that was commonplace at other Japanese prisons. The second year, however, established a steady decline in living conditions, food rations, and medical supplies. The inmates never saw a doctor or a nurse and the medical supplies were meager at best.

Malnutrition and starvation were permanent threats to the inmates' lives. Women's legs became watery, bloated, and painful especially during the nighttime hours. Loss of teeth was beginning to be commonplace. Severe intestinal cramps affected the older inmates doubling them over with excruciating pain. All of the manifestations of malnutrition and starvation were bad enough, but, without doubt, the most dreaded symptom was the frightening specter of blindness that was slowly spreading throughout the prison population.

During the final days of 1944, conditions at the camp had deteriorated even further. If it was allowed to continue much longer it would be a death sentence to all of the inmates. Many of the women prisoners that had suffered the outrages of starvation and an assortment of unattended illnesses were, for the first time, subjected to violent sexual attacks from their Japanese guards. Their commandant established the practice of brutally satisfying their lust. Young and old suffered equally. Even several twelve-year-old children were raped repeatedly.

Suicides were becoming a daily occurrence. Those women who teetered on the edge of sanity, even life itself, were ultimately driven to taking their own lives, seeking release from the pain and humiliation heaped upon them. Some tore at their wrists with rusty nails obtained from the rotting walls of the buildings. Others attacked the guards so that they would be shot or bayoneted. One young girl had climbed to the roof of the barn among the rafters and dove head first into a cement floor.

A number of women died in their sleep simply because they willed themselves to stop living. They had lost the battle and there was nothing left to live for. Everyone existed in a world of weakened will and ebbing physical ability. Hope had died a long time ago and when the sexual assaults started, many were incapable of coping with the terror.

Even Lisa and Madame June believed that the end was near. Every one of the prisoners prepared themselves for that eventuality...

Chapter Three

Late one evening, the moon was partially obliterated by heavy cloud cover. Sporadic showers soaked Jonathon's platoon as they blindly followed the intrepid Sergeant Hammer and his partisan fighters. The rain felt good against the sweating muscles carrying one hundred pound packs as they moved across the terrain just short of a run, hardly a leisurely stroll. The pace was beginning to take its toll on the men, even though they were in excellent physical condition. Every human being had limitations. Sergeant Hammer whispered back through the ranks that they could take a break on the opposite side of the small stream they were about to cross.

The stream contained fast moving water over a base of small pebbles. The men crossed it with ease barely wetting their pant legs. On the far side, Jonathon leaned against a coconut tree and rested. He was an experienced hiker and took every advantage possible to conserve energy. Sergeant Hammer also leaned against the tree. The Rangers were silent. Unnecessary chatter in enemy territory could be dangerous. They followed Jonathon's example and rested. Some ate a Tootsie-Roll candy bar for quick energy. The discipline the Rangers had displayed on the trail pleased Jonathon. He had hand-picked every man for the mission. There wasn't a lemon in the bunch.

"How difficult will it be to neutralize the compound, Sergeant Hammer?" asked Jonathon.

"I've studied the camp from a distance. One thing that is imperative is to isolate the barn and stable where the inmates are housed as soon as possible. There's a Japanese army supply center a few miles from the camp. When they hear gunfire they'll mount an exploratory patrol instantly."

"How many men are at the supply center?"

"Two or three hundred—it varies from day to day," answered Sergeant Hammer seriously.

"My God, the more I hear about this mission the more worried I become," answered Jonathon, shaking his head. His mind raced trying to find some way of isolating the compound from patrols sent from the base. "Would your group of partisans be able to establish a blocking line to contain the patrols so that they don't penetrate as far as the compound? My Rangers can then concentrate on the prison compound."

"I've already taken care of that, Lieutenant. About twenty-five of my best men are scouting for a suitable ambush site and will relieve you of that threat," Sergeant Hammer answered.

"I'm glad you're on our side," exclaimed Jonathon, slapping him on the knee. "We should press on. Too long of a stop will slow us down."

"I agree, sir."

For several hours the Rangers and guerrillas threaded their way through the thick tropical forest and widely spaced coconut groves. Sergeant Hammer grabbed Jonathon's arm and pointed to a break in the vegetation.

"The lights below are from the plantation house," he said in a whisper.

Several lights were visible from the windows of a large building something like a colonial house from his native New England. The men were on a ridge overlooking the prison compound. The ridge was covered with thick undergrowth, concealing them from prying eyes below. Jonathon organized several of his men into a small perimeter defense and told the others to eat and rest and remain as motionless as possible.

He planned to attack at the first light approximately one hour after sunrise. Lieutenant Jacobs and Jonathon huddled around Sergeant Hammer to formulate a plan of action. Jacobs would take two squads of Rangers to surround the prison fence. Once in position, their first job was to take out the four elevated guard platforms at each corner of the rectangular compound. Working in a semicircle they would fight their way in toward the barn and stable building in the corner of the wire enclosure. The plantation house was outside of the fence beside the other buildings. Once the towers were blown, Jonathon and one squad of Rangers would assault the plantation house, neutralizing any Japanese that tried to escape from the building.

Jonathon laid his head against a small log and closed his eyes. He was too keyed up to sleep. Tomorrow would be a rough day for the Rangers. The night was filled with noises from the nocturnal animals who take over the forest after sunset. A soft breeze blew from the west. It felt refreshing against his sweat-soaked uniform. He carefully parted a branch so that he could watch the compound below. The silence of the night was broken by a loud high-pitched scream from a woman in mortal pain followed by several loud commands spoken in Japanese. The screaming continued increasing in intensity. The cry jolted Jonathon's composure to the depth of his soul. He had never heard such excruciating cries from another human being. Suddenly two pistol shots rang out across the landscape. They came from the plantation house. The screams from the tormented woman ceased.

"We've heard similar sounds before, Lieutenant," whispered Sergeant Hammer.

"The bastards are going to pay," vowed Jonathon softly. He had a strong urge to run down the hill to administer justice to the perpetrators.

"Our time will come tomorrow. I pray that the women will have the courage to hold on for a few more hours. Their deliverance is at hand," replied Sergeant Hammer. Jonathon grasped him by the shoulder, glad that the valiant Filipino was with them.

The troops rested for two hours. Just as the sky in the East was beginning to glow, the men huddled around the squad leaders memorizing the sequences of the attack. Jonathon did not say a word to his men. They knew what was expected of them. The gut-wrenching sounds that had emitted from the house filled each of them with a seething rage that made them deadlier than ever. Jonathon had no doubt that they could handle the guard detachments. Each Ranger was equipped with a large supply of hand grenades and extra ammunition for their individual weapons. Most carried a Thompson submachine gun.

The two squads under Lieutenant Jacobs had already left the ridge before the sun rose to get into position for their attack. Once they were in position to wipe out the towers and blow holes in the perimeter fence, their volleys would signal the attack for Jonathon's squad to lunge down the ridge to the plantation house.

A line of coconut trees delineated the fields around the plantation house from the tropical forest. Sergeant Hammer and five of his Filipinos, followed by Jonathon and his remaining squad, crawled to the edge of the clearing close to the house and waited for Lieutenant Jacobs to begin the assault. The main entrance to the house was directly in front of Jonathon. Sergeant Hammer and Jonathon had agreed that they would blow the entrance door with two hand grenades, and enter the vestibule area together. Jonathon would secure each room on the left by rolling grenades through the door as it was opened. Sergeant Hammer would do the same on his right.

Lying in the moist dew-laden grass, Jonathon heard a voice coming from the house. It was a pitiful cry for help and it steeled his resolve.

"No... No... Stop you're hurting me... stop..." It made the hair stand up on the back of his neck. It came from a room to the left of the main entrance. He would have to be careful where he tossed grenades, some of the inmates may be in the rooms.

Two minutes later, explosions took place at the four corners of the compound. Jonathon smiled to himself. Lieutenant Jacobs had coordinated their attacks with precision. He leaped from his concealed position and darted towards the door with grenade in hand. He rolled it at the bottom of the door and flattened himself against the building away from the blast. Sergeant Hammer had done the same on the right side. The door was obliterated. The two men leaped through the opening before the debris had settled. Jonathon held his Thompson at the ready. A door immediately to his left was blown open by the blast. The scene he witnessed sent him into a frenzied rage.

In the middle of the room was a large four posted bed with a lace canopy. A white woman was lying on the bed, spread-eagled with her hands and feet tied to the four corner posts. A naked Japanese officer was on top of the woman with his pants on the floor. Two soldiers were at the head of the bed as if they had been tying the woman's hands. They were frantically reaching for their rifles when Jonathon cut them down with a short burst from his Thompson.

The Japanese officer raping the woman jumped to his feet just as Jonathon caught him with a powerful swipe of the butt of his Thompson. Blood spurted from his mouth and nose as he buckled to the floor at the foot of the bed. Jonathon stood over the enemy officer filled with a hatred beyond anything he had ever experienced in his life. The thought of the cowardly animal forcing himself on the woman tied to the bed unleashed a desire to torment the man the same way the Jap had the defenseless woman. The Jap was probably the camp commandant. He shook his head and tried to get up. Jonathon smashed his boot heel into the man's face and without hesitation fired two rounds into the man's groin. A look of horror and disbelief filled the Jap's eyes.

Sergeant Hammer entered the room and was prepared to run his bayonet through the officer.

"Not this one, Sergeant," screamed Jonathon grasping the rifle. "I want the bastard to live."

"Why?"

"Death would be too easy for the pig. Right now he needs to suffer. It's pay-back time for the little bastard," exclaimed Jonathon in a high pitched voice he hardly recognized as his own.

The woman on the bed began to cry with deep hysterical sobs. Her body wracked with pain and shame. Explosions and shots filled the air from the compound. Jonathon quickly grabbed a blanket to cover her nakedness. "Don't be alarmed lady. I'm an American soldier and we've come to rescue you. These animals won't be able to hurt you anymore. Please, remain quiet until we've secured the rest of the prison compound. Try to understand — you're free. No one will harm you again." He cut the strands holding her feet and arms and tried to reassure her, but she was becoming more and more hysterical. "Don't be frightened lady, you're safe now."

Jonathon turned to look at the Jap officer sitting in a pool of his own blood on the floor. He was shaking all over and managed to sneer insolently at Jonathon, who delivered a vicious blow with this boot to the officer's private parts. "That should wipe the sneer off your ugly face, you pitiful excuse for a man." Sergeant Hammer dragged the Jap officer out the door by the hair and propped him against the side of the barn, and returned to the room.

The woman was in shock. As soon as Jonathon had freed her limbs she began to pound on him, screaming incoherently. "Please lady... Do you understand what I'm saying? I'm an American soldier. You are free," he said distinctly, holding her flailing fists.

27

She was in another world. Her eyes did not look at him; they looked through him. He was concerned about her mental stability and wanted to console her. Yet, he also needed to find out what was happening beyond the walls of the house. If she continued to react the same way, she might hurt herself. He had a feeling that she intended to do just that. In desperation, Jonathon slapped her across the face with an open palm. Her head snapped sideways and she stopped screaming. He felt for her pulse and placed his ear to her mouth. She was breathing heavily.

The small arms firing outside became more intense and much closer. Jonathon glanced at the woman hoping that she would be all right for a while. She was a pathetic looking human being, aged beyond her years with arms and legs the size of a small child. Unconsciousness could be a blessing for her, he thought, leaping through the door.

Chapter Four

Jonathon ran into several of his men from the second squad in the process of mopping up the area between the plantation house and the stable.

"How much of the compound is secured?" he asked.

"The fenced area is cleared, sir," answered a corporal.

"The stable and barn are also secured. Lieutenant Jacob is in there now. We've got a few Jap stragglers to round up. They ran this way into the wooded area where the Filipinos have them surrounded."

"Go get them men. Good work," congratulated Jonathon. The prison had been taken with relative ease. He met Lieutenant Jacob at the entrance to the barn. "You did a great job, Hal. How about casualties?"

"Three wounded as far as I know, Jonathon. The tenacity of the Rangers' assault was partially responsible for the low casualties. We're still sweeping the compound and surrounding area. How many did you find in the house?"

"There were three. Hammer and his corporal checked the balance of the house. I expected more resistance. What's your take on it?" Jonathon asked, checking his watch.

"We caught them just as they were changing the guards. Most of the detachment was in the compound and vulnerable when we struck. Our grenade attack was a complete surprise. Many of them were in the open. Second squad is in pursuit of a few stragglers," reported Lieutenant Jacob.

"As soon as you complete your sweep, Hal, set up a perimeter defense line and use the rest of the men to look after the inmates. Right now I want to get back to the house. I'll talk to you later about it," ordered Jonathon.

"I've got it under control, Jon. God, I'm proud of the men. They fought like demons," added Hal, replacing the empty clip in his Thompson with a full one.

Jonathon ran back towards the house. The Jap officer was still sitting where Sergeant Hammer had deposited him. Tears were rolling down the Jap's cheeks. Years later, Jonathon would often wonder if the tears were a sign of contrition or a submission to fear.

"You'll get no pity from me you bastard. Choices have consequences," Jonathon hollered, running past the Jap.

The woman was still lying on the bed the way he had left her. He made sure the blanket covered her nakedness and checked her pulse. She was still breathing heavily. He pulled out his water canteen to wet a clean handkerchief and began wiping the woman's forehead. She began to move and lifted her eyes to look at him. A shrill piercing scream passed her lips, filled with terror, pain, and outrage.

Jonathon took her two hands and held them so that she could not hit him. He turned his left arm to her so that she could see the badge of an American flag. All of the Rangers assigned to behind the lines missions wore the emblem so that there would be no confusion about their identity. "I am an American soldier. Do you understand?" He pointed to the Ranger insignia and the flag. She did not understand and was still incoherent. "You are free. We have liberated the prison. No one is going to hurt you. Those that have hurt you are either dead or captured. I repeat, I'm an American soldier. Do you understand me?"

Suddenly, a transformation took place before his eyes. The woman was like a cornered animal, coiled and ready to strike out and fight to the death. Perhaps the release that death would bring would have been welcome. For a moment she was confused. The horror that had filled her eyes softened as she focused on the American flag on Jonathon's shoulder patch. The reality of who he was slowly filled her consciousness, and she understood what he was saying to her. His words, spoken in a calm gentle manner, were a source of comfort. Over the years there had been few things that gave comfort. Skepticism and even paranoia helped them from being discouraged by false hopes, and she was afraid to accept what this new discovery meant to her and the other inmates, because she might be deceived. The tension in her body relaxed and large tears began to roll down her cheeks.

"I am an American, too," she said with tremulous lips.

"Don't be afraid. No one is going to hurt you anymore. My name is Lieutenant Jonathon Wright. I'm in charge of a platoon of Rangers that have come to set you free. The compound has already been secured. You are free. Do you have a name?" asked Jonathon, hoping to draw her out in conversation.

"I'm Lisa Carter..." she cried between sobs of relief. "You have seen my shame! The beast would not stop..."

"You fought bravely, Lisa," responded Jonathon. He was relieved that she was able to talk and understand that the prison was now under American control. "I've got to look after my men and see what your companions need for assistance. Are you going to be all right?"

"You've seen my shame," she repeated, hiding her face beneath the blanket.

"I would hardly call it shame, lady. No one could have done more than you did to resist the brutal attacks. I admire your courage and salute you, Lisa Carter. I'll send someone in to help you."

"Thank you, Lieutenant."

Jonathon turned to look at her as he left the room. Her arms were skeleton-like, merely skin over bones! Her uncombed auburn hair was snarled and in disarray. Lisa was still in shock and convulsive sobs continued to wrack her frail body. The shock insulated her from the trauma she had endured. For the time being, Jonathon thought, it was a good thing. His mind was racing evaluating alternatives. If all of the inmates were in the same condition as Lisa Carter, then walking to the coast was out of the question. None would make it half way without some conveyance of sorts, and the Rangers could not carry that many on their backs and still provide protection.

The prisoners were shocked at the level of violence and swiftness of the Ranger's assault on the compound. They were predictably suspicious and cautious in their reaction to their sudden liberation. The Rangers carried three wounded Japanese soldiers to the infirmary section of the barn and laid them on empty bamboo mats. One was the commandant that Jonathon had shot.

When the prisoners saw the Japanese soldiers, pandemonium broke out among them. They attacked the Japanese with feverish ferocity beating and kicking them until they were too weak to continue. One inmate, a tall emaciated middle-aged woman, seized a broken tree branch and began beating the prisoners, swinging the branch like a baseball bat. Jonathan's first reaction was that he should break up the attacks. The women had become a mob and were venting a long subdued hatred. Justice was being served in the only manner available to them. Considering what they had to endure, if he had been one of them, he would have participated in a similar release. The sentence being carried out was commensurate with the terror the Japanese soldiers had unleashed upon the inmates. He deliberately turned his back on the scene and looked for Hal Jacob and Sergeant Hammer.

Small arms fire from the north stopped abruptly. The stragglers had been taken care of. He checked the fenced perimeter noting that Rangers had been posted at strategic points. Sergeant Hammer approached Jonathon with a satisfied look on his face.

"I just received word from a runner. The blocking force has wiped out the detachment at the supply center. We don't have to worry about them now. However, they must have notified other units in the area that the prison was under attack. I've sent patrols to circle the compound for a radius of one or two miles. They'll notify us if there are any Japanese troops in the vicinity," reported Sergeant Hammer.

"You did a great job, Sergeant," said Jonathon sincerely. "I was about to suggest that we send out patrols to warn us of potential counter attacks."

"Could we move the prisoners if I can locate enough water buffalo carts?" Sergeant Hammer asked, anticipating Jonathon's question.

"One thing is certain, Sergeant Hammer. None of the inmates are physically capable of negotiating the terrain on their own. Carts will help but they'll slow a column to a crawl, making us vulnerable to attacks from small groups of Japanese. I doubt if we could make it to the coast before the invasion starts and we would be placing the women at far greater risk out there in no-man's land. Our losses could be heavy."

"Are you suggesting that we stay here until a column can reach us, Lieutenant?"

"I've been thinking about it—unless another alternative offers a better chance of survival for the women in our care. We can set up a pretty strong defensive position right here by shrinking the area we have to defend and wait for relief to come to us," said Jonathon. He had just answered the question he had been entertaining.

"You're probably right," conceded Sergeant Hammer, surveying the compound. "I can set up outposts a hundred yards in front of our defensive line so that we can be forewarned of approaching enemy forces. I am not so much concerned in engaging the forces as I would be in observing them to determine their intentions."

"I appreciate your help, Sergeant," answered Jonathon. "Right now we've got to start taking care of our charges. Where is the nearest water?"

Lieutenant Hal Jacob and the radioman approached them on the run.

"What do you think?" asked Hal, breathing heavily. His dungaree jacket was wet from sweat. "Only half of the woman are able to walk unaided. The enemy dead count is over one hundred."

"We're going to hold here, Hal. Trying to walk out would be ludicrous to contemplate," answered Jonathon firmly.

"We've located a large supply of rice and canned foods in a shed attached to the main plantation house. The mess hall used by the guard detachment is relatively well equipped. Some of the men from first squad are preparing some rice and vegetables to feed the inmates as soon as possible. Rice is a good starter food for them. It'll take a while for them to adjust to eating three meals a day."

"What about medical supplies and other things the inmates need such as soap?" asked Jonathon.

"None, Jon," replied Hal.

They heard the drone of airplane engines coming from the southwest. They scanned the sky and picked up two B-26 bombers approaching the compound at tree-top level.

"So much has been happening that I forgot to tell you, Lieutenant Wright," explained Sergeant Hammer, excitedly watching the approaching planes. "My forces at the blocking position have a radio with them and sent word to our base guerrilla camp that we were in the process of securing the compound. They requested supplies for the inmates and I would not be surprised if we're about to get a delivery."

"My God," cried Jonathon, embracing the intrepid Filipino. "You've made my day. Radioman, try to pick up the frequency the planes are using."

"I've already got it, sir."

The planes began a slow turn around the compound and started dropping bundles from their bomb bay doors and a side door in the fuselage. The sky was filled with parachutes. Soon the ground was covered with supplies. A call came over the radio.

"Air corps to ground. Air corps to ground. Do you read me?"

"This is Lieutenant Wright. We are glad to receive your delivery. I have some instructions I hope you can relay to our control at Sixth Army headquarters."

"Can do, Lieutenant. First I want to warn you that there is a large force of enemy troops about five miles east of your position. They have some tanks and several trucks filled with infantry. It appears that they are headed for the coast. We do not have any ordnance on board."

"Roger, Air Corps. Please relay that *Snapdragon* is going to hold and defend the prison compound. We'll need support, especially if we are attacked by armor. Our charges are approximately seventy women in desperate need of clothing, medicine, and personal hygiene supplies. Do you read me?"

"Perfectly, Lieutenant. We'll relay your message to Sixth Army about the change in plans for *Snapdragon*. Good luck. I will request a recon and support mission for you. You Rangers seem to have the situation under control. Well done, soldiers."

"Thank you, air corps. You've just made our job a lot easier. Roger and out."

The prisoners had stayed in the barn and stable while the air drop was taking place. The large amount of supplies dropped for them, sent a ray of hope and relief through the ranks. They came out of the buildings amazed at the field littered with packages. Jonathon, Hal, and Sergeant Hammer rushed to speak to the inmates. They were gaunt, macabre looking human beings. Their arms and legs were like sticks covered with soiled skin. It was a miracle that they were still alive.

"Ladies," announced Jonathon, waving to get their attention. "I'm Lieutenant Wright of the United States Army. You have been liberated by Army Rangers and some brave Filipino patriots. We are going to stay here until American forces can adequately transport you to a medical facility capable of caring for you. I beg you to be patient for a few more days. We will stay with you and protect you with our lives if that is necessary. I repeat. You are free. The Japanese guards cannot harm you anymore. Some soldiers are preparing a meal of rice and vegetables for you. It will be ready soon. In the meantime, we'll distribute among you the supplies that have been dropped to us. Can anyone tell me where the nearest water supply is?"

An elderly lady with long white hair stepped forward.

"I'm known in the camp as Madame June. Your presence at the camp is an answer to all of our prayers. Thank God you've come! The only water we've ever had came to us through a steel pipe in the stable building. Three of our companions died during the night. One more collapsed and died a few minutes ago when she learned that the Americans have returned to Luzon. It was too much for her fragile system to handle. Would you help us bury them?"

"Yes, of course, Madame June," Jonathon answered, moved by the presence of the frail lady. "When we first attacked the compound and plantation house, we found a woman named Lisa in one of the rooms of the house. She needs someone to help and comfort her."

36

"Thank God she's alive. I was afraid they had killed her. She fought so hard, and has been so strong and brave for all of us... Where is she, Lieutenant? I must go to her," cried Madame June. Her deep sunken eyes stared at him and filled with tears.

"Lisa is in a room on the first floor next to the entrance door," directed Jonathon, turning to Lieutenant Jacob. "Hal, would you look into that water supply? The inmates need food as soon as we can get it to them. After that they need soap and water. We've got to provide some means for them to wash their bodies. This camp wreaks with pestilence. We've got to help them clean it up. I'm going to check out what the air corps delivered."

Six hours after the attack, the prison compound was altered from a sweltering stink hole filled with human beings completely void of hope of surviving the prison experience, to an organized community overflowing with the joy of freedom and full stomachs. Many were at the point where they would have welcomed death, because life was not worth the struggle it took to maintain it.

Lieutenant Jacob had located the water source for the spigot in the stable and the barn. It was a small man-made pond about a hundred feet square. A small amount of water was spilling over the sluiceway indicating to him that it was being supplied by an underground spring. The Japanese had also dug another well close by for their drinking water and food preparation. He and Jonathon figured that they could use the well for the same purpose, and the pond could be used by the inmates to bathe. A young Ranger removed his pants and dungaree shirt and waded into the pond. It was about four and a half feet deep in the center, ideal for the women to use.

Nothing was said to the inmates until the area was prepared. Stakes and wire from the prison fences were erected around the pond by the Rangers. Blankets from the Japanese guard barracks were draped over the wire fence creating a private enclosure for the women. It would be the first time they were free of prying eyes in three years.

A portion of the air drop contained boxes of army pants and shirts that troops wore in the tropics. Socks and assorted shoes were also included. Jonathon ordered them to be displayed next to the enclosed pond so that the women could take a bath first and then dress in clean, dry clothing. The minute they were told what was available for them, the inmates were uplifted. The animated communication among the women was increased as combs, bars of soap, and clean towels were distributed.

The women had already eaten a large serving of rice, peas, and canned pineapple. One of the Rangers had discovered a supply of tea in the Japanese supply room and boiled water to make freshly brewed tea. The tantalizing aroma wafted through the area where the hungry inmates were eating. It was a big hit. Smiles, for the first time in years, appeared on dry cracked lips as they sipped the hot liquid.

A nurse had told Jonathon that the women had lost twenty-five to forty percent of their body weight. The average weight of the prisoners was estimated to be about one hundred and two pounds. The large meal they had just eaten helped to stir the hope that they feared had been lost forever. The food worked its magic, making the inmates more alert and talkative, and thankful for the sense of well-being that a full stomach is capable of producing. Perhaps the tea was more appreciated than the food. It soothed their sensitive stomachs and brought back memories of where they came from and of those who were waiting for their safe return. The near-death stare was beginning to disappear. Their days in purgatory were over.

Chapter Five

Jonathon called the *Snapdragon* controllers at Sixth Army headquarters requesting that additional supplies be air-dropped. He needed more ammunition and heavier weaponry to adequately defend the compound. He also notified them that the inmate's mental and physical health were near the threshold of complete collapse and that additional food was a high priority.

Sergeant Hammer volunteered to ring the compound for up to five miles with his men. That would give the defenders of the prison ample time to prepare for any contingency. Jonathon breathed easier knowing that the intrepid Filipino force constituted the best eyes and ears a commander could have in enemy territory. That would allow the Rangers to concentrate on caring for and defending the inmates.

The women expressed an urgent desire to bath after they had been fed. Jonathon assigned a squad to be responsible for their immediate care and safety. They had completed the privacy enclosure around the pond and had set up a perimeter within the main compound. The inmates would be safe and isolated from any disturbance. Jonathon requested that the sentinels make themselves as inconspicuous as security allowed and to always keep their backs to the bathing women.

The inmates filed towards the pond, anxious to see what had been provided for their use. Soon the small body of water was filled with frolicsome women playing like children at the beach. It was the first time in three years that they had a chance to immerse their bodies in clean water. They did not worry about their safety. The Rangers had wound a net of security around them that contributed to their newly-found sense of well-being. Hope was reinvented. The Americans had returned as General MacArthur had promised!

Each inmate washed and helped those less physically able to do it alone. From the very start, they cared for each other. It had been a mark of their incarceration, no one was left to suffer alone. They had established a fraternity of sisterhood, which acted like a safety net that kept them united against all of the inhumanities the Japanese had heaped upon them. It was a triumph of the human spirit. The chance to bathe and clean themselves ignited that spirit. It was an empowerment that was immeasurable and unconsciously acknowledged by the women bathing away months of Japanese grime. The small pond was covered with three inches of soap suds. The cooling waters had unleashed a new level of energy and joy.

Among the supplies dropped was a supply of combs, enough for each of the inmates. They soon became a treasured possession and were successful confidence builders. The combs represented an important part of their past, and morale climbed instantly when they were distributed. Heavily snarled hair was not easy to comb, but the women diligently kept at the process until their long tresses began to flow about their shoulders.

Madame June, accompanied by Lisa Carter, went to the noisy bathing party taking place within the curtained area. They stopped where the supplies of soap, combs, and clothing had been stockpiled and displayed by the Rangers. Madame June took two towels and two bars of Ivory soap.

"Here, Lisa," said Madame June passing the soap and towel to her. "A bath will feel good won't it? It has been a long time since I felt clean all over."

"It will feel good June, but it can't wash away all the filth the Japanese were responsible for," she replied, accepting the items. Then she ripped the ragged clothes from her body and threw them on the ground. "The beasts can't touch us anymore, thanks to the American soldiers, but how can we ever forget what they did to us?"

"Come now, dear lady. We take one day at a time from now on. Eventually the dark days we've had will become just bad memories. We can't do anything about them now except to grasp for the future. The young Americans have given us a chance to think about tomorrow. The sisters we've buried in the cemetery plot would want us to live our lives in their memory. As for me, I pray that I'll be able to honor their sacrifice by keeping their memories alive."

"You have a nice way of putting things," Lisa answered, following her into the water.

An hour later, Lisa was wiping herself with the clean towel. Madame June was right, she thought. The bath was a cleansing experience, and she was determined to put the past behind her and look forward. Erasing the memories of what the camp commander did to her would not be easy, but she was willing to try. Lisa selected clean underclothes and a set of tan pants and shirt from the supply pile and dressed herself. The simple act of dressing in clean clothing gave her a sense of empowerment and a new feeling of being part of something larger than the encounter she had experienced at the hands of a beast. Once again, she became a human being in control of her life. The immediate rage and pain of the violation against her will was temporarily replaced by a wondrous sensation of being free. She knew that the incorrigible Madame June was correct when she warned Lisa that the ugliness had to be overcome.

Lisa's auburn hair hung below her shoulders after it was thoroughly cleaned and combed. It was thick and sparkled in the mid-day tropical sun as she sat at the edge of the privacy enclosure. She leaned against one of the posts and closed her eyes. From a distance, Madame June saw her relaxing and smiled her approval. There was something wholesome and inspiring about the quiet unassuming Lisa Carter. She possessed an ethereal mystical air that was manifest, yet illusive. Her frail, relatively short stature belied the strong presence she projected. Madame June had recognized Lisa's inner strength and took it upon herself to take special care of her whenever possible.

Throughout their long vigil, Lisa had freely given of herself to those who were sick or were at an emotional low point. She was the steady quiet type who suffered in silence. Few ever heard her complain. When Madame June found Lisa in the room where the young Lieutenant Wright had left her, she was worried about Lisa's sanity. By the time she was able to coax her out of the room with the commandant's blood in the middle of the floor, Lisa had calmed down some. The wise Madame June correctly prophesied that memories of the trauma would most likely be with Lisa for the rest of her life, but Madame June had faith, believing that she had the moral strength necessary to rise above the incident.

Lisa forced herself to think of happier times. Her mind wandered to images she held dear. Vistas of the majestic White Mountains in her native New Hampshire were always a source of inspiration and comfort. Ragged ridges and tranquil valleys filled with thin mists rising from gurgling brooks were precious memories that soothed her soul. If she tried hard enough she could still smell the clean aroma of spruce and fir trees as the winds swept their canopies. She had walked the familiar trails among the towering peaks, with the pungent scent of sweetfern crushed beneath her feet. It would accompany her for miles. She had loved the forest and the feeling of peace and contentment that had filled her heart whenever she walked beneath the arched pathways. It was a sanctuary she had often visited in her youth.

How far away that source of solitude was now! Memories of the mountains and forests had given her the strength to combat the atrocities taking place around her. They had been an oasis of calm in the midst of pestilence and calamity. She found it easy to escape to a time and place of peace and love and beauty. As the years dragged past, Lisa, and most of her companions, had already accepted the fact that they might die in the prison camp. It was a logical, realistic conclusion considering the conditions they had to endure and, in many ways, it made the situation easier to tolerate. All that had changed now. The prospect of eventual deliverance from the camp was a distinct possibility. Their return to civil society, free of war, had been an impossible dream twenty-four hours ago.

Jonathon recognized the inmate sitting with her back against a post near the pond. Her auburn hair was shining in the sun. There was a plaintive far-away - look in her sunken eyes. He was touched by the tragedy they reflected. He slung the Thompson over his shoulder and approached Lisa Carter.

"I see that you've had a chance to put on clean clothes. Is there anything I can do to help you?" he asked in a reassuring voice.

Lisa hesitated a moment. She remembered how he had tried to comfort her. "It is nice to feel clean."

"Have you had a chance to eat something, Miss Carter?"

"Yes, it was a luxury to satisfy our hunger. Thank you for freeing the camp. We were beyond hoping for a miracle, then out of the darkness you appear in answer to all of our prayers. For that, we all owe you a debt of gratitude."

"You and your companions have been an inspiration to me and my men. I can't imagine how difficult your lives have been, and regret that we could not come sooner. We plan to defend the camp until more help arrives. In the meantime, you and your companions should take advantage of this period of adjustment. Eat and rest all that you can. If you need medical attention, the nurses at the barn infirmary have been supplied with most any medication you might need. Be sure to ask them for the vitamin supplements. They'll help your body adjust quicker to the changes in diet."

"There isn't any medicine that can remove my shame," Lisa cried with trembling lips. Her frail body once again was wracked with protest. She avoided looking at him and held her head in her thin, bony fingers, the ugly memories returned with increased fury.

His heart went out to the lady. Jonathon searched for the right words to comfort her and felt helpless: "Let your friends help you, Miss Carter."

"I've been looking all over for you, Lisa," exclaimed a gentle voice. Jonathon turned to see Madame June kneel beside Lisa, cradling her in her arms. "I'll take care of her, Lieutenant. She's had a bad time."

"I'm relieved that you're here, Madame," replied Jonathon, recognizing the elder matron of the camp.

"Normally our Lisa remains on the sidelines, but is always available to help. She's a loner of sorts. When the new commandant of the camp began the unspeakable practice of using the women to satisfy his desires, Lisa was the first to defy and protest against what was taking place. He spoke excellent English. At first Lisa tried to appeal to his honor. She found that he had no honor and punished her interference by using her for the ultimate outrage. He taunted her more than the others... The pig deserved to die a painful death." Madame June kissed Lisa on the forehead and held her like she would a small child.

"The night will soon be upon us," announced Jonathon, surprised to see how quickly the elderly matron defused Lisa's rage. "We'll have to shrink the secured portion of the camp, at least for the night. Can you arrange for the women to remain in the stable and barn? The house may be too vulnerable being on the opposite side of the wire fence."

"I'll see that they settle into their old places for the night," answered Madame June, standing up to grasp his arm. "I don't know how many have said thank you, Lieutenant, but let me say it for all of the inmates. We were existing on sheer will. A few more days with the new commandant would have meant death for some of us, especially Lisa. I have a grandson about your age. You remind me of him. Thank God you came when you did."

"We've been planning raids like this for months, Madame June. When General MacArthur promised the Filipinos that he would return, he meant it. The invasion force is off the coast of Luzon. Soon the island will be free of the yoke of tyranny. We're proud to be part of that force. You ladies here at the camp should rest easy with the assurance that we'll defend this compound against any Japanese attempts to reclaim it. Be patient a little longer. Soon you'll be on your way back to America."

"Your men have been kind and gentle," she replied in that soft way she spoke. "It's nice to see that brave warriors can also be compassionate and generous. The world is going to need those virtues if we're ever going to put this horrible war behind us."

That evening, Jonathon checked the sentry posts within the fenced compound and stationed a man at each of the four entrances to the barn and stable. Their presence was reassuring to the inmates. He knew that his men were stretched thin if a determined attack was to take place. At about eleven o'clock one of the outpost positions let loose with a heavy burst of sustained fire from a Thompson. The camp was instantly alerted to the prospect of an attack, and Jonathon ran to the outpost. The two men at the outpost were lying prone on the edge of their foxhole straining their eyes northward.

"Did you hear anything before you fired?" asked Jonathon, taking a position beside the two men.

"We both saw several Japs at the edge of the sugar cane field. They were advancing in a line with rifles and bayonets at the ready, then we fired at them, sir."

"You did the right thing. I'm going to double check the perimeter. If they make another attempt at this outpost, be sure to give yourselves enough time to fall back to the perimeter line. Don't try to engage them from this isolated position unless you are forced to do so. Okay?"

"Yes, sir."

Every man on the perimeter was alert and eager to get into the fight with the enemy. Jonathon spoke to each man along the line of defense. The young men in the platoon were a hardy bunch with a healthy hatred of the enemy, tempered by the abysmal conditions of the prisoners. If the enemy did attack, he was certain they would pay a heavy price trying to pierce the Rangers' security line. Thankfully, the night passed without further incident.

The next morning, minutes before the sun rose above the mountains, the Japs struck with much screaming and hollering and shouting of obscenities at the Rangers, who met the human wave with determined concentration on their marksmanship. The Japs attacked out of the rising sun which made them difficult to see clearly. Machine guns had been placed on each end of the barn and stable buildings with a clear field of fire. They unleashed a withering stream of death to the attackers. They made the difference. The spirited assault was quickly shattered. Scattered small arms fire continued for another ten minutes. The ground before the perimeter line was littered with the dead bodies of Japanese soldiers.

Jonathan told his men to be on the alert for more attacks. The Rangers were still not equipped to make a determined defensive stand. The only ammunition they had was what each soldier had carried from the submarine. As a matter of fact, they avoided a fire fight whenever possible except for an attempt against the compound. At that point, they would need assistance. Jonathon had his radio man send a call in the clear that they had been under attack and needed supply and possible air support made available to him on demand. Shortly a message was received:

"To the Commanding Officer of *Snapdragon;* Your situation is understood. An air support squadron will be made available to you during daylight hours. Call in the clear on this frequency if needed. We plan to send you more supplies for the former prisoners. If you are in need of immediate medical attention a doctor and a paramedic can be parachuted to you. Congratulations on your speedy capture of the compound. A Ranger company is scheduled to open up a safe corridor to your position immediately after the initial assault units have come ashore. We are cognizant of your situation and will make every effort to safely bring the former prisoners into our lines where they can be properly cared for. Be sure to let them know that the United States has never forgotten their plight. Signed, Lieutenant General Walter Krueger, Sixth Army."

The women had huddled together in the two buildings during the intense fight between the Rangers and the Japanese. They were afraid that the enemy would break through and massacre them all. Lisa and Madame June heard the staccato of the machine guns and involuntarily sought refuge in the far corner of the stable. The eruption of intense fire from the rooftop lasted a short time. Silence and apprehension filled the buildings until the Rangers announced that everything was under control. The Japanese had been stopped.

A few of the Rangers were ordered to leave their sentry post and begin preparing the morning meal. They made a large pot of oatmeal. The night before, they had taken a poll of what the women wanted for breakfast. Oatmeal was an overwhelming winner. Reconstituted powdered milk and brown sugar made a bowl of oatmeal the perfect form of nutrition for the starved women. It was easy to digest and soothing to their shrunken stomachs.

Slowly the defeatist attitude that had existed in the camp was being displaced. Food, soap, clean water to bathe in, and a change of clothes had raised morale several notches. The thought of seeing loved ones in the not too distant future was a powerful uplift. The concept of freedom would have a profound meaning for the women the rest of their lives. It was an emotion and a state of mind they had experienced firsthand.

Chapter Six

Lisa lay on her familiar bamboo matt in the corner of the stable. The food supplied by the Rangers had saved many of her companions who were at death's door. Hope was renewed, yet, some sat at their mats and stared into the darkness of night and the light of day as if they were still witnessing atrocities so unimaginable that their minds had snapped. Rationality was gone and several of the women had ceased to be functional human beings, unaware of the changes the Rangers had made. Their world remained encapsulated in the black recesses of their mind. They were little children once again, lost to the civilized world, perhaps forever.

Lisa felt physical satisfaction about the nutritious food she was able to eat without vomiting. She had forgotten how comforting a bath and clean clothes could be, and was appreciative of the blessings made possible by their sudden freedom. Still, feelings of being violated and unclean remained strong. The terrifying ordeal was passed, but lingering memories of the assault still occupied her mind. Robbed of innocence, sleep had escaped her that first night. It took a while for her to grasp the reality that she had been saved from further violation. Her prayers and supplications had been answered.

Memories of Jeff filled her heart. Lisa and Jeff Summer, her fiancée, grew up in the small community of Twin Mountains, a town on the northern end of the majestic New Hampshire White Mountains. Jeff had been a popular athlete on the high school baseball team. She had attended almost every game he pitched during the four years at school. They had known each other since they were five years old, when they attended Miss Lane's first grade class.

The country was in the midst of a crippling depression for most of their school years. Money and jobs were scarce. The people in the small towns of northern New England fared better than the crowded metropolitan centers near the Atlantic coast. Yankee independence and ingenuity were responsible for feeding and clothing the poorer families that populated the smaller communities. Chickens, pigs, and milk cows were commonly raised to feed the family, and for bartering with others for commodities they had available. Money was scarcer than jobs, so the people lived and survived by being frugal. Few ever felt that they were poor because everybody in town were in the same situation. Those in desperate need was aided by neighbors and friends. Apples, eggs, milk, and potatoes were exchanged amongst the community so that everyone enjoyed a relatively healthy and nourishing diet, free of luxuries.

The tantalizing aroma of fresh baked yeast bread was one of the scents Lisa associated with home. Once a week her mother made a large batch of bread. It was an all day project. The ultimate scent, however, was when the finished dough was baking. Lisa and her sister, Angeline, anxiously waited for the bread to come out of the oven so that they could have a warm piece of bread and butter. Nothing ever satisfied her taste buds as much as the warm bread smothered with melting butter. She often added to the delight by dipping the slice in a saucer of molasses. If there was enough dough, her mother would also make a pan of cinnamon rolls. Even now, years later, she could smell and taste the rolls. Remembering happier times during the long months of incarceration had helped to sustain her mental balance.

The last time Lisa and Jeff saw each other had been an especially poignant time. She had loved him from the first time they walked to school together. He always waited for her at the end of her driveway. They didn't need to talk to communicate. Just being with each other made them happy.

Jeff's childhood dream had been to go to college. After high school he wanted to be an engineer and had won a one year scholarship at Boston University. Lisa enrolled in a small normal school located on Boylston Street while he attended college. She had dreamed of being a teacher like their beloved first grade teacher Miss Lane. She and Jeff saw each other often and explored the wonders of Boston together.

They were small town country people intimidated by the hustle and bustle of the city, yet, there was much about the city that they enjoyed. They attended a Boston Pops concert one evening and continued seeing them whenever they played in the city. The musical experience ignited the passion she had always had for music, especially the piano, which she had been playing since she was five years old. She frequently played at functions in their town and had gained a reputation for her dexterity and versatility on the keyboard. She graduated from the normal school after two years, and with her teaching certification went to work in Twin Mountains as a fifth grade teacher. Jobs were scarce and she was pleased to accept the job offered to her by the school board. She enjoyed working with children, but her true love would always be music.

Two years later, Jeff graduated from Boston University with a degree in mechanical engineering.

The summer of 1941 was filled with anguish and concern with stories of Japan and Germany overrunning their less powerful neighbors. The world was becoming a dangerous place. Jeff graduated with his degree and a commission as a second lieutenant in the army. He had taken the Reserve Officer Training Corps program to help pay his way through school.

Lisa was disappointed that they had to be separated. The world was volatile and the thought that Jeff might become involved in combat was frightening. He tried to assure her that his training would help keep him safe and that when all things were considered, he had an obligation to defend the country they both loved. At the time when Jeff left for duty at Fort Bliss, Texas, Lisa was offered a federal civil service position with the Census Bureau in Washington. It paid more money than her teaching job and would give her a chance to experience Washington, D.C. She became part of a team that was currently preparing for a census in the Philippine Islands, where they worked out of the U.S. Consulate Office.

Before Lisa left Washington, she and Jeff spent a day together touring the city. She could recall every minute of that day with clarity and a heavy heart. It was October 5, 1941, just as the leaves were turning color in the White Mountains, a beautiful time of year. Jeff had called to tell her that he could spend a day with her in Washington.

She watched him step down from the train to the platform of the railroad station. He was standing tall and straight scanning the crowded platform for her. He was a sturdy six-foot athlete with broad shoulders and a ruddy complexion. He smiled often and had a confident air of invincibility. The ready smile and positive disposition were a defense mechanism that shielded a very intense private nature that he shared with few. Lisa had always liked his strong sense of commitment and loved him dearly. He was fun to be with and possessed many of the virtues that were a signature of his generation — honesty, integrity, independence, and the ability to take responsibility.

They toured most of the well-known sites in the city; Lincoln Memorial, Washington Monument, and the Tomb Of The Unknown Soldier. The latter was a sobering moment for both of them. The unsettled world around them did not bode well for the future. Jeff tried to be upbeat and positive that last day, but dark shadows threatened everyone's lives. The future was uncertain at best. They sat on a bench in the magnificent amphitheater of the Tomb Of The Unknown Soldier watching the sentry pace back and forth twenty-one times in tribute to the fallen Unknown.

"Lisa," Jeff began in that resonant voice he reserved for the serious moments in his life. "Things are not looking good in Asia. I wish you were not going to the Philippines. War could break out anytime."

"My director has assured us that the census team going to the Philippines is on a temporary basis. Parts of the American fleet are stationed at Pearl Harbor and will act as a deterrent for the area. I'll be fine, Jeff," Lisa had told him.

He frowned while she spoke. "Nevertheless, I'll worry until you're home again. You and I go back a long way, Lisa. I can't remember a time when I was not in love with you. I want you to know that wherever you go, a part of me goes with you. The future is uncertain right now and whatever happens, remember that I love you. Let's get married the next time we have a chance to be together. I can't imagine a life without you beside me."

"I feel the same," she had replied, kissing him warmly. "I promise to be careful. I'll worry about you, too, Jeff. I'm so proud of you. You're handsome in your uniform. Life is too short not to be together."

They had sealed the pact with an embrace. She could still feel his strong arms wrapped around her. The last time she saw him was at the train station. Tears had filled her eyes. The unknown was frightening and she was reluctant to say good-bye. Jeff had also been silent, trying to be brave and positive. Their world was being torn apart. The premonition each had at their parting would soon come true. Lisa was trapped on the Philippines when the Japanese invaded the islands on December 8, 1941.

She remembered Jeff's last words to her as he turned to her from the train. "My love for you will grow stronger every day we're apart, take care, Lisa. I need you more than you know."

"I love you too, Jeff..." she had answered, amid choking sobs.

The only consolation Lisa had was that during the first year of her imprisonment, the Red Cross knew that she was alive and well at the prison camp. Three years had passed without a word from Jeff or her family. She prayed that the Red Cross had notified her family of her situation, and they would let Jeff know. A few prisoners were exchanged that first year but she was not senior enough to be included. Jeff and her family were in her daily prayers. Now she felt that her dreams and aspirations may be possible.

Lisa thought of Madame June whom she had met only briefly at the Manila Library. She had assisted the consulate in arranging living accommodations for the census workers. She had a large circle of Filipino friends and acquaintances. The war made the census irrelevant. The Japanese occupied the islands and ruled them with a heavy fist. Their cruel and arrogant behavior strengthened the resolve of the native peoples to work for the day when the Americans would return.

The women prisoners were surprised on January 8, 1945, by the sudden appearance of two transport planes flying at tree-top level from the west. They slowed as much as possible upon approaching the compound and opened their cargo doors. Small parachutes began to appear, guiding the suspended packages of food, ammunition, and medical supplies. The ground was littered with bundles and collapsed parachutes. On their return to the west, the planes buzzed the compound low enough for the inmates to see the pilots wave from their cockpit windows.

Jonathon ordered his radio man to send a "well done" to the pilots and ran out to the field to survey the supply drop. Several walled tents had been delivered as requested. He was not sure how long he would have to stay with the women inmates and wanted to get them out of the fetid insect-infested confines of the barn and stable. The tents were a step in making that possible. The women were carriers of every known insect endemic to the tropics, and it was imperative that they begin a rudimentary delousing program. The insecticide and fungicide dusts were also included in the drop, but were pushed from the plane at a distance from the food and medical supplies so that they would not contaminate them.

Before breakfast was prepared, Jonathon asked permission to enter the barn and stable so that he could inform them about what was going to take place. He maintained an alert and secure perimeter with two squads of Rangers and used the third to set up tents and folding cots for the women. He was determined to get them into the tents that day. The squad was also given the task of spraying the women before they could eat or draw clean clothing.

"Please, may I have your attention?" asked Jonathon, standing on top of a shipping crate. "I have some good news to share with you this morning. As you know, planes dropped more supplies today. My men are setting up a delousing station beside the bathing pool. I'd like a few of you to volunteer for the dusting operations. It will be uncomfortable for a while but we want to make sure that your new tent quarters will remain uncontaminated while we're here."

"Lieutenant Wright," announced a voice he had heard before. "I am Madame June. I'll organize the girls to handle the job."

"Thank you, Madame June," he replied, recognizing that the elder lady controlled the camp like a tough drill sergeant. "I suggest that all of you bathe first, and dry yourself completely before you allow the volunteers to dust you. Cover your eyes with a small towel. The men will show the volunteers how to do it. Also, there's enough clothing so that you may burn what you now have on. Select a complete set of fresh clothing after being dusted. Breakfast will be ready immediately afterwards. Any questions?"

"We understand, Lieutenant. Thanks for your consideration and understanding."

"Incidentally Madame June, you may assign women to the tents. We have enough cots and blankets for each of you. I hope you enjoy the new quarters."

"Rest assured we will, Lieutenant."

By late morning the operation had been accomplished. Jonathon watched the reaction of the women. They were all dressed in clean army tans and had been fed another meal of oatmeal, rice, and canned peaches. Some of them were hesitant about the tents. The barn and stable may have been contaminated, but it had been a place of relative security for the past three years. Their reluctance to abandon it was natural, so Madame June spoke to them much the same as a mother would speak to her flock of children.

"All of us have experienced a miracle in the middle of the jungle far removed from civilized society. Clean and airy tents with mosquito nets are now available for our use. What a luxury a cot and clean blankets will be. As we vacate the quarters we've known for three years, we should look upon the transition as the first steps on our way home. I beg of you, don't look back. This morning we're stepping outside of the quarters we've known for three years. It's our first step to freedom. Let's leave the squalor of yesterday where it belongs and take a giant step to tomorrow. Follow me to the tents and don't look back."

The hardy Rangers looked on as the inscrutable Madame June led her companions into the bright sunshine and their new accommodations. Jonathon felt like cheering as the ladies filed past him eager to see what the tents would be like. She smiled and winked at him as she proudly walked by. It was a triumph of the human spirit and it touched all of the Rangers who witnessed the exodus.

Chapter Seven

Large numbers of planes of every description began to fly overhead. Sleek fighter planes could be heard firing at enemy targets as they darted about the landscape. Bombers flew in formation unleashing their bomb loads on enemy troop concentrations, while small planes darted above the battlefield spotting for artillery support. The sound of the heavy caliber naval guns could be heard distinctly from the prison compound. The invasion of Luzon was underway and regardless of the fanatical suicidal resistance of the Japanese, the forces under General MacArthur would prevail. He had kept his promise to return.

Sporadic small arms fire could be heard near the outpost locations where the Rangers and Filipino soldiers intercepted enemy troops in a high state of anxiety and confusion. Stragglers and retreating Japanese soldiers on their way to the interior were not attacking the compound. They simply ran into it without knowing that the Rangers had established a firm footing to their rear.

Jonathon had every man available on the perimeter line. The tempo of gunfire lessened. The radio man motioned to him that he had a call from Sixth Army and passed the receiver to him.

"This is Lieutenant Wright."

"We are sending this message in the clear, Lieutenant," said an authoritative voice. "Operation *Snapdragon* is coming to an end. A flying column is underway to relieve you. A large transportation section will be with the column to evacuate the female prisoners. The column will leave the coast at dawn. Elements of the Twentieth Division are securing both flanks of the relieving column. You are ordered to return to Sixth Army HQ with the convoy. The prisoners will be evacuated to a hospital ship already at anchor in Linguyen Bay. Well done, Lieutenant."

"Thank you, sir. We'll be looking forward to the arrival of the column. Several of the inmates will need immediate medical assistance if they are to survive the ordeal. Over and out." Jonathon turned to his radio man with a grin. "We're going to have company tomorrow, corporal."

Jonathon hastily looked up Madame June in one of the tents erected in a shady portion of the compound. Lisa Carter was with her. They had just completed eating supper and were settling down in the tents for the night. Candles and lanterns were in short supply so the inmates turned in as soon as it became dark. They stretched out on their new cots, covering themselves with the new blankets. They heard the gunfire in the distance and anticipated what it meant. Their ordeal was fast coming to an end.

"Good evening, Lieutenant Wright," greeted Madame June. "The sound of guns and bombs are like music to our ears."

"I've received word that a relief column will be underway in the morning. There will be ample transports and ambulances for all of you. You'll be transported to the coast where a hospital ship is standing by to receive you. The route back to the gulf should be safe. Infantry units will be guarding the flanks of the column. We'll also be accompanying you to the coast."

"Thank you, young man," answered Madame June. "You and your men have given us a reason to be proud to be Americans. Your compassion and generosity are matched by your courage and loyalty. Thank God you came when you did. We owe you our lives. Thank you seems to be inadequate but it comes from our hearts."

"June speaks for all of us, Lieutenant Wright," added Lisa, wrapping a blanket around herself. "I want to tell you personally that I will always be grateful. In the years to come, I'll remember how your calming and reassuring presence at the most terrifying experience of my life gave me hope and comfort. Thank you is inadequate, but, as Madame June said, it's all we have to give."

"You, ladies, are an inspiration to me and my men. I'm glad that your time in Purgatory is about to end. Good night, ladies. Sleep well. Tomorrow will be a new day, one I'm sure you'll remember and describe to your children and grandchildren. We're privileged to have been the instruments of your release."

"Good night, Lieutenant."

Jonathon returned to the most vulnerable and exposed outpost position in the perimeter defense system. Climbing into a foxhole with his radioman and two Rangers, he carefully scanned the open sugar cane field in front of them. He settled in to a comfortable position so that he could observe the field, thinking how much progress the inmates had already made. Nutritious food and clean surroundings were already making a world of difference. He could feel the energy building within the group. Lisa Carter had made remarkable progress since he had found her in the plantation bedroom. At first glance, he had the impression that she was fragile and withdrawn. He now saw her in another light. She was very much a part of the small group of leaders who had guided the inmates through their incarceration. It was her nature to not call attention to herself. Flamboyance and showiness were foreign to her character. She preferred to let her actions speak for her and she guarded her privacy with relentless vigor. She was a very strong-willed person. Her starved body was weak and frail, but her spirit and determination knew no bounds.

Increased naval bombardment announced the birth of a new day. Cooks and servers were busy at work in the Japanese kitchen again preparing food for the inmates. Jonathon remained at the main outpost. During the early morning hours he had spoken twice to the officer in charge of the column on its way to them. The convoy was composed of ten trucks, five half-tracks with quad fifty caliber machine gun mounts and an assortment of ambulances and Jeeps. The task force commander ordered Jonathon to have the inmates assembled with luggage ready to move out as soon as they arrived. The flanking units had run into sporadic opposition. There was a fear that the Japanese would attempt to make a massive all-out attack against the compound to silence the women forever. Therefore, all units involved were at a high level of alert, and the quicker they vacated the area the better.

Once Jonathon received the word he sent runners to the tents to tell the inmates to take whatever personal belongings they wanted, but they would have to leave behind their bedding and food supplies, which could be salvaged at a later date. A loud cheer erupted from the tents as soon as they were informed of the closeness of the rescue column. The exuberance of the women masked the sound of trucks and half-tracks coming through the main gate entrance. Lieutenant Jacob was leading the point vehicle into the compound. They made a U-turn in the sugar cane fields and lined up beside the assembled women. It was a sight that touched the hearts of inmates and soldiers alike.

Those most in need of medical attention were loaded into the ambulances on stretchers. The field was a beehive of activity as the weak inmates were assisted into the two and a half ton GMC army trucks. Strong, willing hands helped them without a word. The soldiers and Rangers exhibited a sense of urgency that the women picked up on and hurried, so as to not hold the column up. The trip back to the coast was not without risk, but there was no doubt in their minds that the strong young soldiers would defend them with honor. The convoy represented a small oasis of America. The women had not gone home to America yet, a part of America had come to them!

Smiles and tears of joy replaced the fear and uncertainty that had dominated their existence. This was the first leg of their homeward journey to families and loved ones. They left the compound with raised fists, loud protests, and profanities. The compound was already history for them.

Jonathon and Lieutenant Jacob kept a count of the inmates as they loaded the trucks. Madame June offered to help them but they insisted that she take her place in the cab of one of the trucks where the seat was more comfortable. When all inmates were accounted for, the order was given to move out. Jonathon and his Rangers took their place in trucks and scout cars at the tail of the column where they choked on the churning dust. A new chapter on the war against tyranny had been written and Jonathon was pleased that *Snapdragon* was coming to a successful conclusion. Long range penetration of enemy lines by a determined number of highly trained soldiers was not a new thing, but a successful rescue of prisoners who would have been massacred by the enemy was a new concept of war in the shadows. The Rangers had exhibited the finest characteristics of the American soldier by cheating the enemy of the opportunity to murder innocent witnesses to their atrocities. A warrior never stands so tall as when he stoops to help a soul in need.

The column of formerly imprisoned woman wound its way through the small Filipino villages on the Gulf of Lingayen. Slowly they came down from the highlands to the shore of the Gulf where the invasion had taken place. As far as the eye could see, ships dotted the ocean from the shore to the horizon. The coastal plain was covered to capacity with mountains of supplies and vehicles of every description. Large battleships and cruisers were firing support missions for the troops ashore. The shells flying over their head made sucking swirling sounds like powerful locomotives traveling at great speed through the air. The shock waves rocked the trucks the women were riding in.

The navy, as promised, was waiting for the women. As soon as they disembarked from the trucks, naval nurses and corpsmen in white uniforms began giving each woman a cursory exam and quiz so as to send them to the proper facility lying offshore. Landing craft with their ramps resting on the beach were waiting to transport them to either a transport ship or a hospital ship, depending on their needs as interpreted by the first line of nurses. The ambulatory patients were immediately sent to the hospital ship by high speed courier boats.

Once on board, the inmates would receive the best medical care available anywhere in the world. Their transformation from prisoners of war to free American citizens was underway. Jonathon and the Rangers stood around the last barge load of women. Responsibility for them had been assumed by the navy. The last two women to board the barge were Madame June and Lisa. They paused to say good-bye to him.

"Well, ladies," said Jonathon soberly. It was a moment he would never forget. "This is where we part company. The best of luck. Our prayers go with you. You're in good hands with the navy. When you get home, have a piece of apple pie and a glass of ice cold milk for me."

"We'll certainly do that, Lieutenant Wright. What will you do when we leave?" asked Madame June.

"I'm a soldier and I follow orders. We've got a war to win. If there are any more prisoners on the islands, we'll do the same thing we did at your old compound. It has been a privilege, ladies. Go home to your families now and put this sordid experience behind you. God bless and bon voyage."

"And may God bless you, young man," said Madame June, embracing him. "Thank you...thank you...." She turned to hide the tears Jonathan saw rolling down her cheeks.

Lisa also hugged and kissed him softly on the cheek. "Good-bye, Lieutenant. We'll pray for your safety. I'll never forget your kindness. Take care of yourself, soldier."

Jonathon touched his cheek where she had kissed him. Suddenly he felt alone and insignificant watching the barge slowly back away from the beach. Lisa and Madame June waved to him as the craft turned toward the large white hospital ship. He looked at his radio man who was also moved by the poignancy of the moment.

"I don't know about you, sir, but I'm going to miss those ladies."

"You're not alone, corporal," replied Jonathon, shouldering his Thompson. "Lets gather up the platoon and check in at headquarters."

Jonathon's platoon fought on Luzon with elements of the 37th Infantry Division in the outskirts of Manila. The initial landings had been relatively unopposed. The deeper they advanced into the interior of the island the more stubborn the Japanese resistance became. General MacArthur ordered the capture of the capital city of Manila as soon as possible. He was returning with an army powerful enough to clear all of the Philippine Islands of their despot occupiers. It would be a costly operation. The Japanese had assembled its finest divisions on Leyte and Luzon under its most fanatical commander, General Yamashito. They fought to the death of every man.

Jonathon and his men were given orders for another perilous mission in the suburbs of Manila. Several road networks feeding into the city proper were controlled by two bridges to the north. Air bombardment was risky for the local population, and would be used only as a last resort. The Rangers' job was to destroy the bridges so that Japanese reinforcements could not enter the city and those already in the metropolitan area could not retreat. Once the enemy was restricted in movement of men and material, they could be eliminated easier by the superiority of American artillery and air power.

The bridges were two miles apart from each other. Jonathon split his platoon into two teams. Lieutenant Jacob would take one team to the closest bridge, while he assumed responsibility for blowing the one further inland. He broke away from the first team so that he could make a wide flanking left hook around the city into suburban sections that were less apt to have concentrations of enemy soldiers. Each team was equipped with three half-tracks with four fifty-caliber machine gun mounts and a radio Jeep. Jonathon rode in the point Jeep with a map and his Thompson on his lap. He selected trails and insignificant roadways in an effort to avoid running into major enemy strongholds. He would need all the firepower and men once they arrived at the bridge. They laid up during daylight hours in an abandoned coconut grove.

As soon as the sun set they drove recklessly along dusty paths toward the main road artery, which ran over the bridge. Late in the evening, they could see the bridge from a hilltop in the moonlight. It was light enough for them to drive without headlights. They approached the bridge with every man's nerves alert and ready. The men and vehicles were covered with tree and brush branches to make them more difficult to identify as American vehicles. There was much confusion in the rear areas of Manila. That fact would aid them.

The task force pulled off into an abandoned road along the river's flood plain close to the bridge without being discovered. They had been lucky so far! They stopped in the shadow of the bridge overhead. One large bridge abutment was right beside the vehicle. Jonathon decided to blow the support with all of the charges they had brought with them. It wasn't necessary to destroy the complete bridge. One failing support would render the bridge useless to the enemy. Not one Japanese soldier could be seen guarding the vulnerable cement pilings. The Rangers worked methodically and rapidly placed the charges where they would do the most damage.

Jonathon looked at his watch. It was getting light. He had plotted their exit route from the area by heading north using a road along the river. He gathered the lead wires and attached them to the detonator. Making sure that the area was cleared, the task force moved as far north as the wire would allow. Jonathon quickly accounted for each of his men, and then detonated the charges.

The blast pulverized portions of the pilings. For a fraction of a second the bridge, heavy with Japanese truck traffic, bowed and swayed when the support failed. A portion of the bridge filled with vehicles crumbled into the river. It almost seemed to be happening in a slow motion film.

The Rangers had watched long enough to see if their handiwork was successful in putting the bridge out of commission. Jonathon yelled: "Let's roll," and climbed in the back seat of the Jeep grasping the thirty-caliber machine gun mount.

Japanese tanks and trucks had set up a roadblock on the path along the river. Jonathon noted a drainage ditch about a hundred yards before the roadblock and directed his driver to take it. The half-tracks would follow. The Jeep engine was screaming in four-wheel drive as they cleared the drainage ditch onto a street filled with Japanese soldiers. Two machine gun emplacements with sandbags piled around them were directly in front of them.

Speed and surprise were all they had at that point. The driver plunged towards the guns at full speed. Jonathon was firing the machine gun as fast as he could at the two enemy nests. The quad fifties on the first half-track also helped eliminate their threat. Seeking some refuge, the Jeep driver turned up a narrow alley filled with boxes and crates. The task force plowed through them. A cloud of dust and splintered wood particles filled the air. They ran close to a building as they exited from the alley.

A Japanese soldier threw a hand grenade at the Jeep as it passed him. The blast caught Jonathon as he was turning the machine gun towards the enemy soldier. The last thing he remembered was a loud noise before darkness enveloped him. The driver was also injured in the blast. The Jeep came to a stop against a utility pole next to the alley. The Rangers in the half-tracks quickly pulled Jonathon and the driver from the smoldering Jeep while they peppered the surrounding area with fifty-caliber bullets, temporarily silencing any resistance. The powerful white half-tracks continued northward as fast as they could. Several miles later, they stopped to care for Jonathon and the driver, lying on the floor of the truck. The driver was dead. Jonathon was bleeding profusely from his upper chest cavity. His right arm and leg were badly shattered and bleeding, but he was alive! They sprinkled the open wounds with sulfa powder, dressing them with compress bandages, and carefully placed ponchos and jackets to cushion his body in the hard riding half-track. They sped at full speed back to American lines.

Jonathon felt the movement of the vehicle and cried out in pain. His first thoughts were of his wife Hope. He repeated over and over. "I'm sorry, Hope… I'm sorry, Hope…"

Chapter Eight

The large white hospital ship with Red Cross markings began to pull anchor and leave Lingayen Gulf. Most of the former women prisoners were being treated deep within the hull of the massive ship. A few stayed on deck to watch the lush green forests covering the hills of Luzon fade in the distance. They had unique thoughts about leaving the place where each and every one of them believed they would die. Mixed emotions ran through their hearts. Most of the former inmates would always carry an intense hatred for the Japanese. They left the island feeling sad that they could not thank the kind, generous, and courageous Filipino people, who had braved death to throw food and clothes over the fence enclosure of the compound. The women knew that without their assistance, survival would have been impossible.

There was a positive side to their incarceration that they could not experience until now. They knew without a doubt that the three years in the prison would be the most grueling test they would ever have to endure in their lifetime. Having survived those tormented years, they privately became proud of themselves. They had found a deep reservoir of strength they never knew existed, and it had sustained them during some of the most difficult trials a human being can be subjected to. If they were capable of surviving imprisonment, they could face and overcome anything life presented in the future. It was a sentiment that touched each of the women, a moment of empowerment that enriched their souls. They had been spared death for some reason and they were eager to embark on the journey of life that lay ahead for them.

Madame June and Lisa sat in two high-back chairs on the main deck near the bridge of the ship. Still dressed in the army tan pants and shirt that hung loosely on their thin, undernourished frames, they rested in the sun breathing the clean, fresh sea air. The gentle movement of the ship as it glided through the water was a new sensation for them. The cool breeze brushed their hair. It felt good to be alive. They were going home, yet home seemed a long ways from the fetid jungles of Luzon. It was a time for reflection and examination of where they had been and where they were going.

"When I get home, I'm never going to leave, not for any reason," declared Madame June, resting her head against the chair back with her eyes closed.

"Where is your home, June?" asked Lisa. She had known the lady briefly before they were captured at the Manila Library. June had been an airline executive for the China Clipper Airways. Her husband had been a pilot for years and had been promoted as executive director for Asian operations.

"I'm from Pennsylvania. My husband Robert and I own a modest home in the small town of Dauphne, a suburb of Harrisburg. I can tell you now that my real name is June Schenk. Bob and I are both from Pennsylvania Dutch families. You saw me in the library, which I rarely visited. That day I was simply returning a book for my husband."

"What a coincidence," said Lisa, recalling that fateful day. "I was reviewing some census material for several of the islands that make up the Philippines. I was a US government census worker. Jobs were scarce before the war. I wanted to be a teacher, but the civil service opening paid more money, so I grabbed it. A year later, I was in a Japanese prison camp. I grew up in New Hampshire near the White Mountains."

"What a beautiful place. Robert and I have visited your White Mountains several times."

"Is your husband still in Pennsylvania?"

"I'm not sure. The first year of our imprisonment, I received a notice from the Red Cross that Robert had been repatriated with a number of British and American subjects. Other than that I don't know if he's alive or dead..."

"I'm sorry, June. I didn't mean to pry. We all have a lot of catching up to do. Now that we're leaving Luzon, I'm a little frightened of the world we have been absent from for three years."

"I've had similar thoughts too, Lisa. My grandson is probably in one of the armed services. Lieutenant Wright reminded me of him. Are you married?" asked June hesitantly.

"No, Jeff Summers and I are not married. We vowed to marry the next time we met. The last time I saw him was in Washington, DC, shortly before the war started. I was on my way to Manila. Jeff had already joined the army. He was a second lieutenant. I have no idea if he's alive or dead or badly wounded somewhere. He must have suffered not knowing what happened to me, although I did send word to him and my family through the Red Cross. Thank God we had them for a while."

"I'm sorry to interrupt you ladies," said a navy nurse. "We've processed most of your companions and would like you to come to the examination rooms. A doctor will be available to you, so feel free to ask any questions you may have. Take your time, we're on our way to Guam, where we'll drop off some of our patients who are well enough to rejoin their units."

Lisa and June followed the nurse to separate examination rooms where they were thoroughly checked by a nurse and a doctor dressed in the whitest linen they had seen in years. Lisa was apprehensive about the physical examination. A young nurse directed her to a chair.

"Please sit down," said the nurse in a calm voice. "I'm Ensign Hanley. I'm going to establish a file on you for our records. My notes have you listed as Lisa. Is that correct?"

"Yes. I'm Lisa Carter."

The nurse asked her to remove all of her clothing so that the doctor could examine her. "I have a hospital johnny for you to put on after you remove your clothing. I understand your reluctance to do that, but the doctor cannot help you unless he examines you thoroughly. Doctor Day is a wonderful physician. You'll be comfortable with him. I'll remain with you." The nurse helped Lisa remove her clothing and saw the burn and bruised markings on her wrists and ankles. "What caused those marks?" asked the nurse.

"The Japanese tied me to the bed... I resisted, but it did no good...." Lisa began to cry. It was painful to think about, and even more painful to describe to a stranger who had no idea what the camp was like. Ensign Hanley embraced the trembling Lisa, holding her until she stopped shaking.

"You're a courageous lady, Lisa. I didn't mean to upset you or have you recall such horrible memories. I can't imagine how difficult it must have been for you. Take your time. Sometimes it's good to let it all out. We're here to help you and no one is going to hurt you again." Ensign Hanley was aghast at the weight loss of the young woman in her arms. Such weight loss in itself was life-threatening. Many of the women admitted that they had probably gained a pound or two since their rescue by the Rangers.

Some degree of blindness afflicted all of the women. The doctors were quick to assure them that as their nutritional needs were met, the symptoms of blindness would slowly disappear. If the sight irregularity did not improve, the ship had facilities to make corrective glasses for those women who needed them. Dentists also joined the doctors in examining each patient so that corrective dental measures could be taken. Tooth extraction was performed on a large percentage of the women. Any type of denture needed by the women could be made on the ship, it was a traveling medical laboratory.

Doctor Day joined Lisa and Ensign Hanley in the examination room. Lisa was a modest person by nature and was very uncomfortable having a strange doctor examine her.

"I'm Doctor Day," he announced, offering Lisa his hand. "I'm here to help you, Lisa Carter. Ensign Hanley has given me the notes she's made about you. I want you to know that I admire your courage, and respect your tenacity to live and survive under the repressive conditions you've experienced. You're a strong person and I admire strength of character. Do you have any questions before we begin our examination?"

Tears filled her eyes again as she looked at the doctor and asked in a beseeching voice: "Is it possible that I'm pregnant...?" The question was filled with all the pain and horror a human being is capable of expressing. Lisa would have fallen off the stool if Ensign Hanley had not been there to hug her once again.

Doctor Day winced at the terrifying possibility and selected his words with care. "My dear lady, I can't answer that agonizing question right now. Try not to worry. I admit, that's a foolish request to make under the circumstances. I want to check you thoroughly so that when we release you from this ship you'll be on the path to normal health with the prospects of living a normal life."

"That doesn't answer my question, Doctor Day," exclaimed Lisa in a hysterical tone.

"I know it doesn't. Of course, I'll check to see if you're pregnant. It will take some time. We may not be able to determine that this early," admitted Doctor Day. "Let me assure you, dear lady, that you're going to get the finest medical care available anywhere in the world. Let's take one step at a time. Right now, it's important that you let us help restore you back to good health. Please, trust me. If tests prove that you're pregnant, we'll cross that bridge when we get to it.

That's easier said than done I know, but it's important for your general health that you try to avoid thinking about things that depress you. Will you try?"

"I'll do my best, but if I am pregnant, will you terminate the pregnancy?" Lisa asked, shaking all over. She surprised herself with the question.

"I can't answer that now," replied Doctor Day. He knew she was going to ask that question and that his answer was inadequate. He intentionally did not tell her that he could not carry out her suggestion unless her health was at risk.

After the physical and dental examinations, the former prisoners were led to a decontamination section where they basked beneath warm, medicating showers. It was a wonderful experience for the women. Some found themselves singing and humming beneath the relaxing nozzles. It had been three years since they enjoyed the luxury of a shower. Brand new clothing was provided from underclothes to blouses and skirts and white socks and low tennis shoes, for wear on board the ship.

At the end of the evaluation and shower routine, the women were then treated to a haircut. Several nurses had volunteered to act as hairdressers. The doctors insisted on having their hair cut as short as the individuals would allow. The short hair was easier for them to maintain and treat for insect infestations. The haircut was a health-related operation instead of a stylistic statement. The procedure started with a shampoo before the cutting and one after the haircut to insure that all insect infestations were eradicated.

The women continued their slow journey back to the individuals they had been before the war. Red Cross officials had interviewed each of them, so that their relatives could be informed of their release from the Japanese prison camp. They ate meals specifically designed for them that were tasty, nutritious, and easy to digest. The smell of brewing coffee and fresh baked bread stimulated their sense of smell. Once their digestive system became used to processing food normally their diets would change. They ate larger than usual servings at a sitting. The galley stewards enjoyed watching them eat. The most popular food was ice cream. It was the food they dreamed about in the hot sultry jungle. The stewards were happy to supply their fill. Most people take food for granted, but these women would never become that complacent again.

The attitudes of the former prisoners were changing with every mile the ship sailed towards home. Anticipation of going home and knowing that their loved ones had been informed of their rescue was a tremendous lift to their morale and dispositions. In between sessions with the doctors, dentists, eye specialists and internal medicine specialists, the women were quick to adapt to life on the ship. Magazines and newspapers were devoured page by page. They caught up on the current war news. The invasion of Europe seven months previous to their release from prison was greeted with great enthusiasm. Movies were a favorite pastime.

The women packed the movie auditoriums every day. Movies such as *Going My Way, Jane Eyre, Casablanca* and *Gone With The Wind* helped them make the transition back to normal life. Some of the movies made them cry openly in the auditorium.

Their prison experience was something that would always separate them from mainstream citizens. It conditioned every aspect of their lives, and defined them as human beings. Food would never be wasted; clean water would always be a luxury; fresh air would never be taken for granted again; and the greatest gift of all, freedom, would always be treasured. Three years of their lives had withered away almost as completely as their bodies. They had a lot of catching up to do, but time would never be frivolously wasted again. The sheer pleasure of being alive, with a full stomach and a promise of more in the future made it the most precious gift of all. Life had meaning at last!

Lisa's auburn hair had been cut just below her ears. The naval-nurse-turned-hairdresser suggested that with her round face, she would look good in bangs. Lisa agreed, not caring much how it was cut, as long as it was free of lice. The end results drew compliments from her companions. She looked at herself in the mirror. Her eyes were still sunken deeply into their sockets. They stared back at her with a hard disinterested look as if she were a stranger. Her Jeff would not know her now. Her protruding cheek bones gave her an unearthly look. The few days of a normal diet had improved her appearance, but she had a long ways to go to be the girl Jeff remembered.

On the second day at sea, Lisa walked about the ship. At first it was difficult to coordinate her steps with the slow rhythmic movement of the ship as it cut through the southwest Pacific. Time and practice gave her confidence. The solitude of the sea was a source of strength to her. Its immensity and its infinite moods reminded her of the green spruce-fir forests of her beloved New Hampshire. They evoked the same kind of emotions. Lisa's first sunrise and sunset at sea were a revelation. She never knew such spectacular panoramas of color existed. The beauty exceeded a sunset in the White Mountains. The sun colored the entire sky from horizon to horizon. Small isolated cumulous clouds floated in a sea of color. It was the most beautiful sight she had ever seen and it touched the creative and artistic elements of her makeup. It made her feel alone and a melancholic sadness filled her heart. Beauty always made her cry — tears came easily.

The magnificence of the scene rekindled her belief in a just God. During the long years in prison, she had given up and believed that He had forgotten them. Not once did God give her, or any of the other prisoners, a sign that He loved them. She had been a firm believer and was deceived by His absence. She could believe again if He would give her a sign explaining why the women were allowed to suffer for so long.

What lesson was there to learn from such brutality? Answers were still wanting!

Lisa leaned against the rail watching the blue water being parted by the passage of the ship. Two smaller coast guard ships maintained a course and speed abreast of the ponderous hospital ship. She had been told that there was a danger of enemy submarines. It seemed to her that the smaller ships had intentionally positioned themselves to intercept a torpedo if one was launched at the hospital ship. The willingness of the coast guardsmen to place themselves in danger to protect others was an act of courage that brought tears to her swollen eyes. She thought of the young Ranger, Lieutenant Wright and his men who had placed themselves in harm's way to free and protect them. Were such acts an instrument of God's plan? She believed it could be so, and found comfort with that knowledge.

The sound of a piano being played somewhere on the ship broke her reverie. She followed the sound and arrived at a recreational room with several wounded soldiers in it. The piano held her transfixed. She had not played or heard a note of music for three years. A wounded soldier with one arm missing was picking out the melody of a song popular before the war, *September Song*.

An urgent desire to play the piano grasped her. She stood beside the soldier and listened carefully. He noticed her presence and stared at her stark appearance.

"It's a beautiful song isn't it?" asked the soldier. "I used to play quite well they told me. Now I'll never be able to again..." He looked at his empty sleeve with sad eyes.

"I remember the song," said Lisa. "You do it well with one hand."

"Do you play?" he asked.

"I used to. I haven't seen or heard a piano for three years," she confessed.

"Please, take my seat, lady. You never forget if it's in your blood."

"You're kind. I had no intention of interrupting you," replied Lisa.

"I was just killing time. Please try it out," the soldier vacated the seat and motioned for her to take it.

Lisa was nervous and shook all over. She flexed her fingers and ran them over the keyboard doing the scale several times. The soldier watched with interest. She closed her eyes and concentrated on a song she had loved to play, *Clair de Lune*. The melodies came to her as soon as she touched the keys. Small thin fingers ran up and down the keyboard giving the song life and heart. The song touched the soldiers and others in the room, and moved her to tears. She didn't know how much she missed music until this moment of discovery, three years hence. She played *September Song* for the soldier. He turned away from the piano to hide his own tears.

Lisa played several of her favorite classical pieces, such as Chopin's *Polonaise*. Everyone in the room now flocked around the piano. Some were in wheelchairs. Loud whistles and cheers erupted when she stopped. Opening her eyes, Lisa saw the people around her and smiled. The power of music was limitless. The soldier with one arm listened in awe to her performance.

"Lady, I'll give up the piano anytime to you. You were magnificent. Thank you for playing."

Lisa nodded her head in acknowledgment and suddenly felt hot and weak. She was burning up and began to shiver. She got up from the piano and fainted. Perspiration streamed down her forehead. She was having another malaria attack.

Chapter Nine

The cavernous hospital ship dropped its anchors in Apra Harbor off the coast of Guam, an island west of the Philippines and part of the Mariana Islands. Lisa sat in a wheelchair on the top deck of the ship with several of her women companions. She had suffered a relapse when the malaria attack seized her two days ago. High fever, severe chills, and profuse sweating and dehydration had drained her resistance and energy. Lisa was at a weaker and more vulnerable state now than she was when she left the prison compound.

The staff had worked diligently to bring her fever down with cooling baths. She was already in a weakened condition and the staff was afraid that the trauma of the malaria attack might be more than her body could handle. They were quick to hook her up to maximum glucose intravenous feeding and administered massive dosages of quinine and some of the more modern medicines to halt the disease and ultimately cure it, as long as she did not return to the malaria-infested area of the tropics. For two days she was too weak to walk.

The fever and chills produced intense headaches. Every muscle and joint in her body ached and her abdomen felt as if it were on fire. She was a very sick person and the doctors were concerned about her ability to resist the ravages of the disease. It was not uncommon for additional attacks to take place every three or four days.

While the ship was resting against its anchor chains, a two-engine Catalina float plane landed in the calm waters of the anchorage. The women clearly saw the pilot and waved as the plane settled in the water and taxied to the amphibious ramp on shore. The ship was in the process of discharging a hundred soldiers that had been treated for minor wounds and were capable of returning to active combat duty. The nurses told the women lining the deck rails what was taking place and announced that a few severely wounded men were going to be brought on board for transit to Pearl Harbor.

Lisa looked out over the rails wearing the sunglasses the doctor insisted she wear to protect her already weakened eyes from the harmful rays of the tropical sun. The malaria attack had deteriorated her sight even more. She saw the island of Guam as a green mass of land without any distinctive definition. Everything looked fuzzy to her. She was able to see the plane as it landed but could not distinguish the pilot.

The breeze was brisk and chilled Lisa as she wrapped herself tightly in the heavy white robe she wore. She was uncomfortable most of the time, either too hot or too cold. Finding a suitable balance between the two extremes was difficult. When she was cold, her body began to shiver and shake until her teeth rattled. About the only thing she could do was sleep, which her body desperately needed to successfully fight the disease. Lisa asked the nurse to wheel her back to the ward so that she could lie down.

The Island of Guam was a busy communication and supply center. There was a small detachment of American troops stationed on the island since it was taken from the Japanese a year ago. It had been an American protectorate before the war. A large United States flag proudly waved from the roof of the large building at the amphibious ramp where the Catalina float plane was being secured to a dock. Four seriously wounded soldiers were onboard, including Lieutenant Jonathon Wright. He was unconscious when they left Luzon and was still unconscious as the sailors lifted him from the fuselage of the float plane. They temporarily deposited him and the other wounded men in an infirmary where they were checked by doctors and nurses from the hospital ship. It was a precautionary move before loading them on a landing barge for transfer to the hospital ship.

Jonathon was sheathed in white linens and strapped securely to a stretcher. Doctor Day took his pulse and checked his heart. A small bottle of glucose and blood plasma were hanging from a post attached to the stretcher. Doctor Day asked one of the nurses to replace both intravenous bottles before the men were transferred. So far, Jonathon seemed to have made the trip without any complications. As soon as he was placed on board the ship, Doctor Day and others would be able to make a more detailed evaluation.

An hour later, the soldiers were in examination rooms deep in the hull of the ship. Its powerful engines began their distinctive hum and lifted anchor. Its destination was the Pearl Harbor anchorage on the island of Oahu. The trip would take up to two weeks. Jonathon and the other soldiers were examined thoroughly by the ship's staff. He remained unconscious. His next in command, a burly staff sergeant, had petitioned their commanding officer to write up Jonathon's performance on the raid for the Medal of Honor. He had led the raid from the front with competence, displaying a courage and daring that stirred his men to maximum efforts. His calm leadership under extreme conditions was a source of inspiration. He led by example instead of by command, and his men followed him with assurance. He had a reputation for being creative and clever. The men were saddened to leave him at the aid station. The scuttlebutt was that the wounds would very likely terminate his army career.

The aid station and a regimental operating center had stabilized Jonathon so that he was no longer bleeding through the wounds on his right arm and leg. Torn flesh wounds were dusted with sulfa powder and quickly dressed. The open wounds of his leg and arm would require X-rays before surgery could be performed. Broken bone pieces were removed where possible, but no effort was made to repair the bone damage until it could be adequately assessed at a more advanced facility. Morphine was generously given to Jonathon to relieve the pain that accompanied the massive trauma he had sustained. It could be addictive, yet, its superlative power to make pain disappear had few equals. Glucose and blood plasma were immediately administered intravenously at the field aid station, a decision that probably saved his life.

When the ship's surgical team removed Jonathon from the stretcher, they were alarmed that he had been bleeding so extensively. The bedding was saturated with blood. The surgeons quickly stripped Jonathon's clothing and the dressings that had been applied, so that they could evaluate his condition. He presented a challenge to their dedication and skill.

The humerus, the main bone in his upper arm, was broken in several places and completely shattered at one end so that it would never be able to restore itself. The ulna and radius bones of his lower arm were also broken but had not been disintegrated. The surgeons agreed that reconstruction had to be done immediately, and they fashioned a stainless steel rod to help hold the humerus in place. Luckily, his elbow joint and wrist had escaped serious injury. They dressed the wounds after removing all of the broken fragments of shattered bone and placed temporary casts on the upper and lower arm so that his elbow and wrist could not be moved.

The most severe damage to Jonathon's body was to his right leg. It looked to the surgeons as if a sharp knife had cut away all tendons and tissue. His kneecap was destroyed and the femur (thigh bone) was broken in two places. The fibula and tibia (bones connecting the knee to the foot) were also broken in several places. Steel pins were used to secure all of the leg bones and to repair his kneecap. The surgeons were most concerned about the ability of his body to replace the lost muscle and flesh in his thigh. They spent hours reconnecting the torn tendons and blood vessels, and debated about leaving portions of his leg free of any solid cast so that they could begin skin grafting procedures soon. Finally, a cast was fashioned to be strong enough to hold his leg in position without undue movement, leaving portions of his thigh open. A cast around his ankle and foot was held in position with temporary rods running from the cast on his knee to the foot, and from his knee cast to a cast fashioned around his pelvis.

Jonathon's upper torso was covered with superficial cuts and abrasions that had bled extensively. They were sterilized and dressed with heavy compress bandages. His upper body was wrapped with several layers of bandages to help the ribs mend. He also had two broken ribs. They would be a source of pain and shortness of breath, but they were far from being as serious as his leg injury. For ten hours the surgeons labored over his broken body. The consensus was that Jonathon's army career was at an end. Neither the arm nor the leg would heal completely.

A radio dispatch filled with information from the four soldiers' record files was sent to the ship from Pearl Harbor, where main records were kept. Most of the information was routine. There was a special attachment added to Jonathon's files:

First Lieutenant Jonathon Wright has been nominated for the Medal of Honor for action behind enemy lines in Manila. The awards section of the Army was being notified so that appropriate investigations can be carried out to verify the accuracy of the nomination. Regardless of how the nomination goes, Lieutenant Wright is a very brave soldier." Signed, Major General Arnold Hayes, USA, Executive Officer Special Operations, Sixth Army.

A week later when the hospital ship was halfway between Guam and Pearl Harbor, they experienced a submarine attack. The protective convoy of two destroyers and two coast guard cutters had located an unknown submarine trailing the convoy. The escorts formed a security ring of vessels around the hospital ship and began dropping depth charges. The destroyers and cutters were like charging mustangs as they were pitched and tossed in the heavy wake of the powerful ship of mercy. They were trying to protect it and at the same time trying to eliminate any threat to its safety.

Lisa was watching the small escorts when a torpedo hit a cutter and almost broke it in half. The light cutter lifted out of the water and buckled from the impact. Lisa saw the explosion and screamed. She saw two bodies being flung into the air as if they were rag dolls. They landed in the oil-soaked water, which instantly burst into flames. She started to cry, horrified at the fiery death of the brave coast guardsmen.

A second torpedo fired at the cutter missed and came within inches of hitting the hospital ship in the rudder. The remaining destroyers and cutter unleashed a blanket barrage of depth charges that produced a powerful muffled explosion below the surface. The water rose in a fountain of spray filled with bits and pieces of the enemy submarine. Diesel fuel spread on the water as secondary explosions followed in quick succession. The hospital ship launched several small motor boats from the lower deck to help look for survivors from the stricken coast guard cutter. Before the small boats were in the water, the two pieces of the once proud cutter disappeared beneath the water.

Anxious spectators stood in awe at the sudden eruption of the violence that consumed a ship and its crew. The recovery launches picked up only twelve men from the smoking debris field. Over one hundred men went down with their ship! The magnitude and severity of the catastrophe overpowered their imagination. They wept for the brave men who were protecting them from the same fate. It was a scene etched on their souls that they would carry to their graves.

Lisa became hysterical and had to be comforted by her companions. June Schenk found her at the railing and took her in her arms. Large tears formed in Lisa's eyes, and dropped on her cheeks. June held her and placed a handkerchief in her hand. Lisa's malaria attack had given all of them concern that she might suffer long-term ramifications from the high temperatures. She was slowly overcoming the effects of the malaria attack and her weight was increasing at about a pound and a half per day. The doctor insisted that she continue using the wheelchair so that she could conserve her energy. They were pleased with her recovery; it reflected a strong constitution and a firm resolve to get well.

Good food and proper medicine were working their magic. Lisa's eyes reflected the progress she had already made. The dark discolored sections of skin under her eyes had disappeared and the lines about her face had begun to soften and would soon vanish as she continued to gain weight. She wheeled her chair through the women's wards, talking with them and playing cards. She especially liked the movies being played every evening. It eased her transition from prison camp life to normal existence, but the piano was the biggest factor in her quick response to the care the navy lavished on her. The daily piano recitals were gaining a wide circle of admirers, who flocked to the lounge when the word went out that she was playing.

Lisa also rolled herself through the men's ward on the same deck. She was shocked at the severity of their wounds and at the large number of young men, most younger than her, who would carry ugly reminders of combat for the rest of their lives. She thought she would find a gloomy atmosphere in the wards, but to her delight, she discovered that the men were playful and positive instead of morbid and negative. They laughed and kidded each other a lot and encouraged those who were on the brink of giving up. No one was allowed to suffer alone. The way they rallied around their more severely wounded buddies was an inspiration to Lisa and others who witnessed the close bond and positive spirits in the face of massive human suffering. She often played cribbage with the men. It helped all of them pass the time.

One day after the torpedo disaster, Lisa was wheeling her chair through that portion of the men's ward near the nurses' station, where patients in need of intensive care were placed. One of the patients had not moved or talked since they had placed him in the ward. Out of curiosity she checked the clipboard hanging at the foot of the bed and saw the name, "Lt. J. Wright." She looked closer at the patient's face to see if it was who she thought it might be. His right leg was suspended slightly off the bed and was wrapped in several layers of sheets. His arm and shoulder were covered with a plaster of Paris cast. It was the same man she remembered. His eyes were closed, and he looked pale and drained. She drew closer to the side of his bed and spoke softly to him.

"Can you hear me, Lieutenant Wright?" she asked. It was hard to imagine that this was the same soldier who had captured the prison compound and set the women free. She was saddened to see him lying so still and so severely wounded. It didn't seem fair.

"Do you hear me, Lieutenant Wright?" she asked again.

This time he opened his eyes to see who was calling his name. He blinked several times, as if to see her better and still did not recognize her.

"Yes, I hear you," he answered with a thick tongue, slurring his words.

"Don't you recognize me?"

"No," he replied, blinking his eyes again. He still had a terrible headache. "Are you my nurse?"

"No, do you want her?"

"Yes," he struggled to answer.

"I'll get her for you," answered Lisa. She wheeled to the nurse station telling them that Jonathon wanted something.

"He's probably got a headache," commented the nurse on her way to Jonathon's bed. "He's in a lot of pain. He may never walk normally again. The doctor said they may have to amputate the leg if it doesn't respond to medication or if gangrene sets in."

"Oh, no," cried Lisa.

"Do you know him?" asked the nurse.

"He was the Ranger who freed our prison compound," Lisa told her, remembering how Jonathon and his men had given a new life to the compound as soon as they arrived.

"There was a note attached to his records. He's being nominated for the Medal of Honor for action behind enemy lines in Manila. That's where he was wounded. I understand that his men brought him to the coast," said the nurse.

"I'm not surprised to learn that about him," answered Lisa. "He's a very special person."

Doctor Day walked into the nurse station and saw Lisa talking to the duty nurse.

"Miss Carter," he announced. "I'm glad that I found you here. Would you please come with me? I want to discuss something with you."

"Yes, Doctor Day," she answered with a tremor in her voice.

They entered the nurses' room where the Doctor closed the door behind them and took a seat beside Lisa's wheelchair.

"I've just come from the pathology laboratory where I read the results of the latest urine test we've been conducting," explained Doctor Day with a serious look on his face. "The most recent test confirms that you are pregnant!"

Chapter Ten

A high pitched scream passed Lisa's lips as she collapsed in her chair. Doctor Day had anticipated such a reaction to the devastating news, and his heart went out to the modest young woman. He was uncertain just how he would react to the information if he had been in her shoes. First, she had to suffer the physical and emotional trauma of being brutally violated by an enemy soldier, and now, she was faced with the prospect of being reminded of the assault every time she looked at the child she was now carrying in her womb. Doctor Day had waited to inform her until he took a second test to confirm what the first one had told him. The tests were conclusive. The Japanese soldier had left her with a child!

Doctor Day was prepared to let her know that he could legally perform an abortion on her if the pregnancy threatened her health. It was a difficult judgment call. Physically he did not foresee any problem with her having a normal pregnancy and delivery. What bothered him the most was the fact that over a long period of time the spiritual trauma could be destructive to her health and mental stability unless it was handled in a very positive way. If the child was going to be an object of hate and potential abuse he thought that it might be the best for all concerned to terminate the pregnancy, the sooner the better.

Lisa began to stir and picked up her head off the arm of the wheelchair. Doctor Day called a nurse to help him transfer her to a cot. He took her pulse. It was racing wildly. She opened her eyes and looked at the nurse and Doctor Day standing over her. Without a word, she swung her feet over the edge of the cot and reclaimed her chair. There was a calmness about her that defied description.

"Can I get something for you, Lisa?" asked the nurse.

"I'm all right thank you. May I speak to the doctor alone, please?"

"Of course," answered the nurse leaving the room.

"I'm sorry to be the messenger of bad news," confessed the doctor, checking her pulse again. It was close to normal.

"I've been expecting it, Doctor Day. I had a premonition about it. If I asked you to give me an abortion would you do it?"

"Under the circumstances, yes. If this is a course you want to take, I suggest that it be done as soon as possible. Don't even think about having it done by some quack in a deserted back alley room. There's always a risk with any operation. Having it done under the most antiseptic conditions decreases the chances of anything going wrong."

"I understand, Doctor Day, and thank you for making that option available to me. I haven't made up my mind yet, even though I've been thinking of little else," answered Lisa. "What would you do if you were me?"

"I'm not qualified to make that decision for you, Lisa. We have several chaplains on board, would you like to talk with one?"

"Yes, I would like that," she replied.

"I'll see that one looks you up shortly. By the way I noticed that you know our new patient, Lieutenant Wright," said Doctor Day.

"He and his men liberated the prison," answered Lisa. "How badly is he hurt?"

"His right arm and miscellaneous cuts and bruises will most likely heal with time and therapy. His leg is in horrible condition. By the time we reach Pearl Harbor, we'll know whether to amputate or not. If not, his chances of regaining one hundred percent usage are slim. The explosion could have killed him. He's a lucky soldier."

"Thank you, Doctor Day," said Lisa, ready to leave the room. "I'll give you my decision within a few days. My immediate thought is to ask you to take me into the operating room before anymore time passes. Now that my condition is a fact, I have some reservations about that first impulse. To be honest, my hesitation surprises me."

"Whatever you decide, young lady, I'm sure it will be the right thing for you. I admire your courage. I'll send the chaplain for you."

"Thank you, doctor."

Lisa slowly wheeled her chair back into the ward. A nurse had just left Jonathon's side. He was terribly pale. Heavy lines around his eyes and mouth made him look old. Lisa stopped beside him. He opened his eyes and saw her.

"Are you the one who spoke my name?" he asked in a strained voice as if he had a sore throat.

"Yes, it was me, Lieutenant. Don't you recognize me?" Lisa questioned, wheeling closer so that he could see her better.

"I'm afraid I don't remember. My head has been mixed up lately…"

"I'm Lisa Carter, one of the women inmates at the prison on Luzon."

"Now I remember," Jonathon replied, studying her face and noting the different haircut. "The changes are becoming to you, Lisa Carter. What a coincidence that we should meet again under such different circumstances…." Jonathon's voice became weaker and weaker, and he closed his eyes.

"Rest well, Lieutenant."

A Baptist minister wearing a naval chaplain uniform intercepted her in the hallway as she left the men's ward.

"Excuse me. I'm Reverend Matthews. Are you, Miss Lisa Carter?"

"Yes."

The Baptist chaplain was a man in his late forties with gray hair around his temples. He was tall and thin with big brown eyes. There was an air of serenity about him that Lisa felt immediately.

"Doctor Day suggested that I get in touch with you. Why don't we go to the chaplain's office near the chapel on this deck?"

"That will be fine with me," answered Lisa nervously.

"Your prison internment must have been a terrifying ordeal for you. It took great courage and a strong will to survive it for three years. I'll pray that you get well soon and return to your loved ones as quickly as the navy can get you home. Are your legs injured Miss Carter?" asked Reverend Matthews looking at the wheelchair.

"No, I had a severe malaria attack and Doctor Day insisted that I use the chair until I've regained my strength. Do you know why Doctor Day asked you to see me?"

"Yes I do. What a terrible dilemma you face. I pray that God can give you guidance to make the right decision and the strength to live with the one you will choose. Human life is a gift from God."

"Are you trying to say that God sanctioned the way I became pregnant?" Lisa asked defensively.

"Not at all, Miss Carter. I simply wanted to say that life is sacred and that God loves all of his children."

"Even the deranged Jap that raped me?"

"Even him, as hard as it is to accept."

"If He's a benevolent God, then why did he allow such an act to take place?" she cried out in desperation.

"I can't give you an answer that will make sense to you, Miss Carter, or give you the solace you deserve. We humans don't have all the answers. However, God has promised us that He will never give us any burden too heavy to bear without granting us the strength to carry the load."

"If your wife was raped by the same man who raped me, would you agree for her to have an abortion?" Lisa asked.

"You ask that question in anger and with justification. As a man, I'd probably want an abortion to end the pregnancy. As a man of God, I know that all life is sacred, even newly conceived infants, and man does not have the power to determine who lives and who dies."

"You can't answer it for me can you, Reverend?"

"Not the answer you're looking for, my child. I understand your pain and anguish. Please pray with me," pleaded Reverend Matthews, taking her hands in his. "I believe that God has tested you enough and will help you find a solution to the dilemma."

He kneeled beside her on the floor and in a gentle voice asked God to grant Lisa peace of mind and strength to make the right decision and the resolve to live with that choice. Lisa left the chaplain's office filled with mixed emotions. She was hoping for a clear plan of action, and ended up with more questions and indecision than ever. She believed in Jesus Christ and accepted Him as her Savior, the same as her parents. The sacredness of life was a concept that she had always accepted; however, she questioned that sacredness when life was created by a barbarous act against a woman's will. It was not enough to admit that life was sacred. Where was the justice and restitution for such an act? The commandant had received quick and just consequences from Lieutenant Wright's hand. The other inmates had administered the ultimate verdict. Justice had been carried out, but it was not enough for her... She wanted revenge and it was not available to her!

Lisa wheeled to her bed in the ward. How nice it was to climb into a clean bed with white sheets again. She felt exhausted. Much had taken place and she needed some quiet time to reflect on what she was going to do. Jeff weighed heavily on her mind, wondering what he would think about her bringing another man's child to their relationship and future marriage. She understood what a staggering fact that would present to any man who had been fighting the Japanese.

June saw the troubled look on Lisa's face. "Are you all right, Lisa?" she asked.

"That all depends, June."

"What do you mean? You look different! Has anything happened to you?"

"Yes, I'm pregnant," Lisa snapped back. "The pig got me pregnant, that's what's wrong."

"Oh, my dear girl," cried June.7 "I never thought about that possibility."

"Well, the doctor has confirmed it. If you were me, what would you do, June?" Lisa asked defensively.

"That's not fair, Lisa," responded June, pulling a chair next to the bed. "If I were you, I'd probably be more despondent than you appear and I'd be seriously considering ending the pregnancy. I understand it's much easier the first month. I visualize a lifetime of trying to justify a son or daughter with Japanese ancestry, knowing that your generation has had thousands of young men and women killed and maimed by the Japanese in this war that is not over yet. Believe me Lisa, a generation of people are going to hate the Japanese for the war they started and the Americans they've killed. They won't want anything to do with the enemy. Have you given any consideration that your child would grow up in an atmosphere of hatred and distrust?"

"You present a valid and accurate point of view. Sure, I've thought about those things and a whole lot more," answered Lisa with a sigh. "I keep asking myself why it had to happen to me."

"Of course you do. I'd think the same things. The answer to that question is found in our faith. If you are selected to carry this to fruition, then God must feel that you have the courage and will to do so. Perhaps He has more faith in you than you do yourself."

"The chaplain told me the same thing," Lisa told her, closing her eyes. "By the way, Lieutenant Wright has been wounded and is in the ward on this deck."

"I have not heard that," replied June. "I must visit him and see that the girls do the same. He seemed so formidable and invincible."

"He's looking quite the opposite right now. I'm tired, June," Lisa said, closing her eyes.

"Of course, Lisa. Rest well, my dear."

The next day, Jonathon woke up listening to beautiful music that filled his ears. He looked around and saw no radio nearby and rang for the nurse.

"What can I do for you, Lieutenant?" asked a nurse.

"Am I hearing things, or is that music that I hear, Ensign?"

"It's coming from the recreation lounge down the hallway. It's beautiful piano playing isn't it? Would you like to be wheeled down there so that you can see what's going on?"

"That would be swell, Ensign, but I don't want to be a nuisance."

"It's no problem, Lieutenant. I'll get an orderly and we can navigate your bed down the hallway. All of your intravenous tubes are attached to the bed so that it can be moved. Hang on a second."

A few minutes later, Jonathon was wheeled into the recreation room. The nurse turned his bed so that he could see Lisa playing the piano.

"Thank you, Ensign. She plays very well doesn't she?"

"She has attracted a large audience of listeners whenever she comes to the rec hall. It's so nice to hear beautiful music fill the wards. The lady certainly has a talent for interpreting the pieces she plays. If I had the time I'd stay and enjoy it with you, Lieutenant. When you're ready to return to the ward, have someone call us. It's nice to see you alert this morning."

Lisa still played with amazing dexterity. She had been afraid that it had been lost during the three long years of absence from a piano. She was filled with joy to discover that her heart and fingers could still be in synchronization with each other, interpreting the music as she perceived it. There was a powerful softness and gentleness to the music as it filled the hall with graceful harmony. She had not lost the ability to transmit the images and moods reflected in the pieces she selected. She had a passion for the piano classics of the masters such as Chopin, Rachmaninoff, and Beethoven. Her audience in the recreation room were young adults and she chose pieces they would be more familiar with: *Una Paloma Blanca*, *September Song*, *The Twelfth of Never*, *Red Sails in the Sunset* and her all time favorite, *Clair de Lune*. She even played some boogie-woogie, which drew claps and whistles from the crowd.

For almost an hour Lisa played non-stop, without the benefit of sheet music, while sitting in her wheelchair with a pillow for proper height. Jonathon watched her every move and marveled at the intensity of her playing. She succeeded in transmitting the feelings and emotions the composers wanted to evoke. It was a wonderful musical experience that elevated their thoughts and hearts from the every-day commonplace to the sublime.

Chapter Eleven

Lisa sensed the involvement of the listeners, and a wonderful feeling of peace and contentment came over her. She had rediscovered the power of music to enrich the human spirit and, at the same time, found a part of herself that had been dormant for too long. She had a gift for musical interpretation and intensity of involvement that few professional musicians are privileged to possess. Lisa ended her playing with tears streaming down her face. She was pleased that the people in the room liked her playing, but she was especially thankful for what the music did for her. She had arrived at a decision that would affect her for the rest of her life. The music had given her the courage to accept the consequences. It was a moment in her life that she would always remember.

Lisa announced that her last selection would be an old Irish folk song called *Danny Boy*. When she had finished, cheers and claps filled the room. She turned her wheelchair to face the audience and bowed modestly, moved by their enthusiasm.

"Thank you. I'm so glad you liked it. It's been a long time since I had a chance to play." Tears of joy and discovery filled her eyes, she blushed shyly. She noticed Jonathon's hospital bed near the door, and directed her chair towards him.

Jonathon was smiling at her. "Your performance at the keyboard was fabulous, Miss Carter."

"Thank you, Lieutenant. You look much better today. I hope your recovery will be complete," said Lisa, eyeing

Doctor Day standing in the doorway. "Here comes Doctor Day."

"I was worried about your absence from the ward, Lieutenant," announced the doctor. "Now I find you in here listening to another patient of mine, Miss Carter. Isn't her playing something special?"

"It sure is, doctor," Jonathon agreed.

Lisa blushed again. "Don't you know that flattery is the last resort of fools?"

"Well, it's true, Miss Carter. Your playing has lifted morale on this deck fifty percent. I heard most of your selections down the hallway. I love your rendition of *Clair de Lune.*"

"I'm glad you liked it, doctor," replied Lisa.

"I came looking for you, Lieutenant, because there's a launch bringing an investigative officer aboard. He wants to speak to you about the Medal of Honor. Are you prepared to meet with him?" inquired Doctor Day, as he checked Jonathon's pulse and heart rate.

"I hate to admit it, doctor, but I'm not very strong. My headaches are still as severe as ever. There are bits and pieces of the raid that are still fuzzy to me. I'll do my best though," Jonathon answered in a weak voice.

Lisa watched Jonathon close his eyes. "I have to go now. Madame June has told me that she'll be looking in on you from time to time. Thanks for being such a good listener, Lieutenant. Good-bye, Doctor Day."

"I'll see you around, Miss Carter," replied the doctor. "There goes a remarkable young lady. Conditions at the prison must have been atrocious. Most of the inmates have progressed beyond our expectations."

"Miss Carter has improved a lot..." Conversation was making Jonathon weary. "Would you take me back to the ward, doctor? I'll see the awards officer whenever he's ready."

"I'll tell him, Lieutenant," assured the doctor, pushing the bed towards the doorway. "I could stall him off until tomorrow."

"I'd appreciate that, Doctor Day," answered Jonathon, closing his eyes and turning his head to a more comfortable position on the pillow.

That next morning, pain still wracked Jonathon's body. His left side felt as if it was on fire and every movement he made, within the confines of the hospital bed, increased the pain. He rang for the nurse and explained how he felt. She wiped the beads of perspiration from his forehead and stuck a thermometer in his mouth.

"You're running a fever of 104 degrees," the nurse announce in a calm deliberate tone. "Drink all the water you can for now. I'm going to get Doctor Day. Have you had malaria?"

"Not that I know of," answered Jonathon, taking a swallow of cold water from the glass the nurse held to his lips.

"Rest easy, Lieutenant. I'll be right back."

"I'm not going anywhere, nurse," Jonathon responded in a weak voice.

A badly wounded soldier at the opposite end of the ward began to scream loudly. He was protesting the decision to cut off his severely shattered arm. He was a farmer and needed it to run his farm when he returned home. Jonathon heard Doctor Day's reassuring voice trying to calm the young soldier.

"I understand your position, Sergeant, but if we don't amputate soon, you'll die from gangrene that has started to spread already. Do hear me?"

"No," screamed the disagreeing sergeant. "I... I...."

A few minutes later, Doctor Day stood over Jonathon checking his pulse and temperature one more time. The doctor's normal jovial demeanor was shaken enough that even

Jonathon, in his feverish condition, recognized his sober mood.

"How old is the sergeant, doctor?"

"He just turned twenty, Lieutenant. The longer this war lasts, the younger the wounded men are. He'll be out for awhile. I've scheduled him for surgery this morning. Now, Lieutenant, I'm commencing stronger antibiotics to control your infection. The weakness and sore aching body you feel are caused by the infections somewhere in your wounds. Drink all the liquids your bladder can hold."

"I'd just as soon stay away from that addictive pain killer stuff," Jonathon protested. "If you don't mind, I'd prefer old fashioned aspirin. If it doesn't work, I'll try the stronger stuff."

Doctor Day admired Jonathon's strong constitution. "I agree wholeheartedly, Lieutenant. The nurse will be in shortly. I'm due in the scrub room. The awards officer is on board. Anytime you feel like talking to him, let the nurse know."

"Thanks."

Later that afternoon, Jonathon awoke from a long nap. His headache had disappeared and the pain in his leg and arm was less acute. The fever was three degrees less than it was before Doctor Day prescribed antibiotics, and he was hungry for the first time since he had been wounded. The nurse offered him a chocolate frappe with an extra scoop of ice cream. It tasted good, satisfying his hunger and soothing his parched throat. Feeling much better, he told the nurse that he would see the awards officer.

Once again, sounds of piano music wafted through the ward. Every patient that was awake cocked their heads to listen to the medley of folk songs played by Lisa Carter. Jonathon listened carefully to the light touch the former prisoner had on the piano keys. She rarely pounded them, even when playing difficult classical selections. Lisa had the gift of conveying the struggle between love and anger; happiness and despair; and choices and consequences. There was something captivating about her style that allowed the listener to become a part of the music, no matter what type she selected to play. He heard her play an old favorite of his, *There's A Gold Mine In The Sky*. It brought memories of happier days in the rural town of Monson.

"You have a visitor, Lieutenant Wright," reported a nurse, interrupting his pleasant reverie.

"Thank you, nurse."

A heavy-set infantry officer stepped into Jonathon's line of vision and introduced himself. "I'm Captain Gaines, awards officer for Sixth Army."

"Glad to meet you, Captain. Pull up a chair if you can find one. I'm not sure that I can contribute anything that you don't already know," declared Jonathon.

"Actually, Lieutenant, I'm most interested in your perception of the escape once the bridge was blown. As you know, all recommendations for the Medal of Honor are thoroughly investigated so that the deeds of the men involved rise to standards established by congress for the medal." Captain Gaines paused a moment, noting the severity of Jonathon's wounds and continued in a measured, precise tone. "By investigating each case thoroughly, the Medal of Honor continues to be the most coveted award in military history. Many are chosen but few succeed in receiving the medal. The fact that every man in your raiding party recommended you for the award speaks highly for your courage and dedication to the mission. I salute you, Lieutenant."

The two soldiers talked for an hour and a half. Jonathon explained what they did and why he handled it that way. He ended the interview with the following observation: "If I'm worthy of the medal, then every man in the task force is entitled to the same treatment. They took the same risks I did and fought just as tenaciously. Without them, the raid could not have been conducted. If the medal is awarded to me, I want it understood by everyone concerned, that I'll wear it only on the condition that it is shared by the soldiers who carried out my orders. They saved my life by bringing me out of the battle alive. My driver lost his life in the same blast. It would be unfair to his memory if the medal was only for me."

"I applaud your strong feelings, Lieutenant, and I'm inclined to agree with you. I've been doing this job now for two years and I'm still in awe of the inherent courage of the American soldier. It's been a pleasure, Lieutenant Wright." Captain Gaines stood up and moved his chair out of the way. "I wish you a speedy and full recovery from your wounds."

"Thanks for stopping by, Captain," said Jonathon, closing his eyes, leaning back against his pillow. The medal meant little to him. His final statement to the Captain was true. Seconds later, he was sound asleep.

Lisa continued to play the piano and rest as the hospital ship slowly plowed through the deep waters of the Pacific towards Pearl Harbor. Physically she was feeling stronger by the day, and her eyesight was improving so that she only used the magnifying glasses to read. Every waking moment she deliberated over the decision she had to make. Some of her dreams were filled with grotesque images of people with Japanese facial features.

One night she woke up from a nightmare depicting her stomach full of large blood-sucking worms. She screamed and screamed and pounded on her stomach to kill the slimy crawling creatures. Talking to the chaplain did not help her. She had the feeling that he had little empathy for how she thought about the situation. Time was running out and a decision had to be made.

She meticulously evaluated every aspect of the issue using her own standards of right and wrong. At times she was afraid she was going mad. The baby growing inside of her was becoming a tortuous burden. One day she wanted to be free of it and the next day she would hear the lonely cry of a baby in her sleep. She woke up filled with doubts. The dilemma was consuming her. Days went by with no clear resolution to the problem. Lisa experienced a turning point in her deliberations one day when she and Madame June visited Lieutenant Wright in his ward. They were permitted to wheel his bed onto the deck so that he could be in the sun and watch the ocean.

"I really appreciate a chance to get out of the ward," Jonathon said. He was still being heavily medicated with antibiotics, but he was improving. His color was near normal and his appetite was increasing daily. "When I see how badly some of the men are wounded, I feel fortunate. Just being able to eat a normal meal when I'm hungry is a blessing. If I ever cease to be thankful for all my blessings, then God should punish me."

"We'll be in Pearl Harbor soon," said June, checking the blankets around Jonathon. "We don't want you to catch a cold, Lieutenant."

Lisa was quieter than usual. She had become more withdrawn since Doctor Day informed her of her condition. She had shared it only with June, who understood her wide mood swings.

"I expect we'll be parting company at Pearl. I'm not sure if I'll be held there until I'm recovered or shipped on to the States," Jonathon wondered aloud. "My wife, Hope, has probably been notified of my wounds."

"Where is your home, Lieutenant?" Lisa asked, thinking how his wife must be worried about him.

"I grew up in Monson, a small town in northern Maine. My wife and daughter live there with my parents."

"We're practically neighbors," exclaimed Lisa, thinking how appropriate it was that he was from northern New England. "I lived in Twin Mountains, New Hampshire."

"I thought I detected a down east accent," Jonathon smiled at her.

"You must miss your wife and daughter," inquired June.

"I haven't seen either of them since late 1941. Faith was only six months old at the time. She's the joy of my life. She won't know me when I get home," Jonathon said with a sigh. "Life took on a new meaning for me when she was born. Without children, we don't reach our full potential. Hope claims that she would be lost without the baby to care for. Little children are our hope for a better world." Lisa and June saw the tears forming in his eyes. Suddenly he looked tired and drawn.

"Why don't we take you back to the ward, Lieutenant, so that you can rest easier." June and Lisa directed the cumbersome bed toward the door. Jonathon was overcome with memories of home and family. Lisa excused herself after they had placed his bed in the ward.

Touched by his devotion to his wife and daughter, Lisa reflected on his comments about the value of children. Normally, she would have agreed with his assessment, but her situation was unique. A child should be the product of a man and woman in love with each other. Was it fair for her to bring a child into the world without a father to love it? Also, was it fair for her to subject a child to ridicule and possible hatred because of its ancestry when the child had nothing to say about that? These questions ran through her head hourly without any answers.

After hours of praying and deep self-analysis, Lisa arrived at a decision. Five minutes later, she was sitting in Doctor Day's office. He led her into the examination room and gave her a thorough physical examination. She had come to respect the kind and gentle doctor and was prepared to share her thoughts with him.

"I've reached a decision about the baby I'm carrying, Doctor Day," she announced with a tilt of her chin. "I've decided to keep the baby. I know that the father was a contemptible beast, but the child cannot be held responsible for him. I have the power of ending a life or giving it birth. It will be my responsibility to not only give the child birth, but to love and nurture him or her. I believe the child deserves a chance to live. There has been so much death and destruction these past few years. Maybe I'm making a mistake, but since I've made up my mind, I've found a peace and sense of self-worth that is comforting to me."

Doctor Day calmly listened to Lisa's explanation. Tears welled in her eyes. He hugged the fragile lady and passed her some tissues. "Let the tears come, dear lady. Your decision has confirmed my faith in mankind. What a glorious day this is! I understand how agonizing your decision has been, and I agree with you one hundred percent. I also know that your decision may cause you pain and anguish at times. From what I've been able to observe, young lady, I believe you have that reservoir of strength to rise to any challenge. I have two favors to ask of you, Lisa."

"I'll answer them if I can." She wiped her eyes.

"Would you consider it out of line if I asked you to be the child's Godfather? And would you keep me advised of how things are going for you? This war isn't going to last forever. When it's over, I plan to return to Boston to resume my practice. Will you extend me and my wife the privilege of being friends? I would also consider it a privilege if you would allow me to be your family doctor!"

Chapter Twelve

Five years later — June 24, 1950

Lisa and her four-and-a-half-year-old son, Terry, were riding in her 1947 Studebaker Champion automobile on their way back from Boston to Lisa's childhood home in Twin Mountains. Her mother and father had passed away while she was in captivity during the war, and her sister Angeline had maintained the family homestead since their death. When Lisa returned home at war's end, Angeline insisted that she live in the house.

Lisa looked at her young son sleeping on the seat beside her and took his tiny hand in hers. The small boy reflected his Japanese heritage with angular facial features and eyes, though they were softer than a pure-blood Japanese. He was a Eurasian, a half-breed with Asian and Caucasian blood. Lisa did not see the Japanese heritage when she looked at him, instead she saw a product of her womb. She had given him life and nurtured him and was teaching him the values she lived by. The only thing Japanese about him was his eyes. Beyond that he was as much American as any child in his kindergarten class at Twin Mountains. Regardless of how others perceived him, Terry was her pride and joy. He gave meaning to the difficult years she had spent since being released from the prison camp on Luzon.

She defended him as much as possible from despicable and hurtful remarks made by adults or children. Many World War II veterans carried a deep-seated hatred for anything remotely Japanese. Some referred to him as a little "Jap" and were contemptible of his presence. Other epithets were like "slant eyes," "Tojo" and one with frightening connotations for Lisa was "hara-kari." Few of the younger children who called him that understood the meaning of the words, but they were applied to him just the same, simply because he was different.

Terry was told at an early age what the derogatory name-calling words meant. Lisa made a point of informing him why others perceived him the way they did and emphasized that it was not him personally that they hated. Lisa knew that Terry was too young to understand. She maintained a very protective cocoon around him, intentionally avoiding large crowds or gatherings where Terry might be the target of ridicule, such as restaurants and supermarkets; consequently, they lived a rather reclusive life. He deflected unkind remarks with all the pride his mother had taught him, and would reply: "I'm an American!"

The measure of protection Lisa could wrap around Terry was limited when he was allowed to have social interaction with children his own age. As a matter of fact, Terry handled the barbs of racial prejudice from children his own age with an amazing attitude of tolerance and forgiveness for a five-year-old. Obviously obnoxious people were avoided whenever possible. Lisa's hopes and prayers during those youthful years was that eventually, people would accept him on the basis of his character and integrity instead of the heritage he was not responsible for. She had dedicated herself to preparing him for the moment that she was certain would come someday.

The sun had just settled in the west as they passed through Manchester on their way north. It was just as well that Terry had given up and fallen asleep. Tears filled Lisa's eyes and rolled down over her cheeks, dropping onto her new green blazer. For the past nine years of her life, tears had frequently flowed. Wiping her eyes so that she could see the road clearly, Lisa recalled events that led to one of the most painful experiences of her life. It had all started when she left the hospital ship at Pearl Harbor.

June Schenk's husband had met the hospital ship as it docked at Pearl Harbor Navy Base, prepared to take her home to Pennsylvania. The former prisoners were held over for another week while being interviewed by navy and army intelligence officers and historians. All were given government vouchers to purchase new clothing and personal items. They were also tested and extensively evaluated to be certain that all that medical science could do for them was carried out. On the trip from Luzon to Pearl, the former prisoners had gained an average of twenty pounds each.

Doctor Day insisted on being Lisa's physician. When June and her husband were ready to leave Hawaii for the homeland, Doctor Day signed Lisa's release so that she could accompany them to the states. Lisa could still hear his kind and encouraging words.

"Good luck, Lisa Carter. Hold your head up high and never let anyone judge you by the child you carry. Don't ever let anyone judge you who has never been tested to the degree you and your fellow prisoners have endured for the past three years. I've given you my address in Boston. I hope you'll look me up when this ugly war is over. Go home now, dear lady, and put your life in order." He embraced her like a father would a daughter and wished her a "Bon Voyage."

Lisa traveled to Philadelphia with June and her husband. It was a tearful parting at the train station. The two women had been inseparable during their incarceration, and Lisa soundly believed that she owed her life to the gentle and resourceful matriarch. An hour after she waved good-bye to June and her husband, Lisa boarded a train bound for Boston. The army headquarters at Pearl Harbor had given her Jeff's address and location. The army also told her that they would send a special communication to Jeff's commanding officer requesting that Jeff be sent home on a short furlough. They had forwarded her reservation itinerary to his command post. She was excited about seeing him. Her first visit with him in Boston was an experience she still could not believe. The hurt still lingered.

Jeff had been promoted to captain and was busy training his company for combat. He had been alerted about the time her train would arrive in Boston. It pulled in at six o'clock in the morning. Jeff made sure to be there when the train rolled to a stop. He instantly recognized Lisa as she stepped down from the train. Her auburn hair was cut short just below the ears, the way she had worn it when they were going to school. This meeting, the first in four years, was the fulfillment of all their dreams and prayers. They embraced with an intensity reserved only for those who have teetered on the edge of life's volcano and survived.

Jeff had borrowed a friend's automobile, a 1941 Buick sedan, and had parked it close to the station. He released her and told her that he had a vehicle. Once outside, he pointed to the car and opened the passenger door for her. He was like a little kid on his first date. His Lisa was alive and with him. He could hardly believe his good fortune. Now, anything was possible! He mentioned that he had only a twenty-four hour pass and limited coupons to purchase gasoline, so they decided to go to a nearby restaurant where it was quiet, spending hours reminiscing over steaks and coffee. Late in the afternoon, they ended up at a park near the Boston Shell beside the Charles River. They talked about changes back home. Lisa's parents had caught pneumonia and passed away a few months apart. Lisa told him that her sister Angeline lived in the old house with her husband, Harry Lender. He had been medically discharged from the navy when he lost a leg on a destroyer that was torpedoed in the North Atlantic early in the war.

Lisa held back from telling Jeff about her condition until the last few hours of his leave time. She did not want to spoil the rapture of the moment. The scene that took place was etched in her memory.

"Jeff, I have something important to tell you," Lisa began in a tremulous voice.

"What is it, Lisa?" Jeff asked, perplexed at her somber tone.

"On the last day at the Japanese prison camp, I was raped by a Japanese soldier…" Lisa stopped to catch her breath and searched for the right words to lessen the impact of the message. "As a result of that attack upon me, I'm pregnant!"

"Pregnant with a Jap kid?" he cried incredulously.

"Yes, Jeff… a Japanese…" Lisa heard the tone of his response and began to cry, afraid that she was going to pass out. She had trouble breathing and gasped for air. Jeff pulled away from her as if she were a leper. His revulsion horrified her.

"I can't believe that a man can impregnate a woman if she doesn't want it," he cried, disbelieving her story.

Her world was crumbling around her. Jeff was like a stranger! The look in his eyes made her feel dirty and cheap. "I could not help it, Jeff," she talked fast to defend herself, frightened of what was taking place. Jeff had changed! She was stronger than ever since her release from the compound but she was still relatively fragile. Several times she reached out to Jeff for physical support and was rejected each time. She felt weak and the fear of fainting and falling to the ground troubled her. Lisa was completely unprepared for his vitriolic response to her situation. She clung to a nearby tree for support and faced Jeff.

"What are you going to do about it, Lisa?" he demanded in a high pitched voice. "You can't have the baby. We're at war with Japan. It's unthinkable."

"It's unthinkable… yes… but it's a fact, Jeff," she pleaded for understanding and begged him for some comfort, a touch, a kind word, anything to stop feeling dirty and immoral and cheap. She never dreamed that her Jeff could abandon her so abruptly and so ruthlessly. "I'm not to blame, Jeff. You have to understand what it was like..."

"Are you going to keep the baby?"

"Yes, I've decided to have the baby. I had hoped that you would support me in that decision," she anxiously cried.

There was a long pause. Jeff avoided eye contact with her and spoke in a softer tone. "Do you realize what you're asking me to do? I don't think I could ever condone your decision to keep the baby. Under the circumstances, I think it's insane and unfair to you, me, and the child."

"Maybe I was wrong, but I expected you to support me, Jeff. I need your acceptance so badly. You'll never know how much I've agonized over the decision. I won't change my mind. Sure, I've thought of all the problems it could cause. I was hoping that our love for each other would be strong enough to overcome any obstacle," she pleaded one more time.

"It is, Lisa. I've been true to your memory and I'd do anything... but accepting a Japanese baby... I, I just can't believe you'd ask such a thing of me."

"Well, Jeff," cried Lisa, desperately drawing from her last vestige of strength. She presented an ultimatum to him. "Where do we go from here? It's now or never, and it's up to you, Jeff."

He was unapologetic. "I can't imagine being with you, while you're pregnant with someone else's child. Don't you know what you've done to us...?"

Jeff never finished the sentence. Lisa, consumed by rage and pain, slapped him hard across the face. "How dare you blame me for my condition, how dare you? I expected more than this from you, Jeff. The memory of our love for each other gave me courage over the years when it was a rare virtue."

Lisa turned from him and ran hysterically across the park, anxious to get away from the stranger that Jeff had become. In the distance she could hear Jeff calling to her. "I'm sorry, Lisa. I'm sorry, Lisa..." He stood his ground watching Lisa run away from him without any attempt to stop her. A lifetime of dreams had just been obliterated!

Lisa pulled the faithful Studebaker to the side of the road to wipe her eyes. It was a traumatic experience that still hurt. That reunion with Jeff five years before had shattered her sense of trust and belief in close friends. She never saw Jeff again. Something had changed him, and the agony she felt still lingered. It was difficult for her to accept that she was alone.

Terry was sleeping on the seat with his feet resting on her lap. She brushed a few loose strands of hair from his face and patted him on the cheek. She loved him more than she could ever say, possibly because a few in the world hated him for what he looked like. Occasionally, when she was confronted with negative reactions, the thought would quickly run through her mind that maybe she had made a mistake bringing him into the world. Fortunately, those kind of thoughts never lasted too long. Just thinking about them angered her.

Lisa pulled back onto the highway remembering all that had happened to her since she returned home from the war. She had lost Jeff, a large part of her world, but she had gained a staunch supporter and a personal friend in Doctor Day and his wife, Erin. Terry was born October 10, 1945, two months after the war. Doctor Day had been discharged from the navy and was continuing his practice in Boston at the Mass General Hospital. When her time was close, he strongly urged Lisa to come to Boston so that he could deliver the baby. She was relieved to oblige. The kind doctor was a man of his word. He and Erin became Terry's Godfather and Godmother.

That was the beginning of a friendship that was instrumental in guiding Lisa through parenthood without a husband. She taught the fifth grade at Twin Mountains Elementary School during weekdays. One weekend, when Lisa came to Boston with Terry for a checkup, Erin Day had arranged an audition for Lisa with the Pops Orchestra. Erin was an enthusiastic supporter of the orchestra and knew Arthur Fiedler, the conductor, personally. Erin and the doctor offered to babysit Terry while she kept the appointment for the audition.

Fiedler was impressed with Lisa's talent. She lacked the touch of professional discipline, but she made up for that deficiency by her unique interpretation of the musical selections. To many in the hall during that audition, it was as if they were hearing the music for the first time. It had a deep fresh appeal that touched emotions and feelings. They loved her simple style without frills. "Music with heart," was the way Fiedler had described it.

Soon, Lisa became a regular performer and soloed frequently. She was especially adept at accompanying singers and soloing violinists. Her modest and serious demeanor quickly earned the affection and respect of all of the orchestra members. She was a good team player.

Life had been difficult those first years after the war. She recalled being in a constant state of exhaustion, with bills adding up to more than her teaching salary could pay. As soon as she accepted the weekend positions playing with the Pops, her financial worries lessened. During the summer months, she stayed in Boston so that she could participate in the performances at the Shell beside the Charles River. The Fourth of July performances were her favorites.

Her sister Angeline attended every performance and insisted on looking after Terry during rehearsals and evening performances. Terry enjoyed the experience. With each passing year the boy absorbed the sights and sounds of the people of Boston celebrating their country's birthday. On

Terry's fourth birthday, he was old enough to understand the role his mother had with the orchestra. He was proud of her. During the 1949 Fourth of July performance, Terry sat in front of the Shell with his Aunt Angeline. He saw his mother wave several times to him. He beamed all over, and returned her wave.

When Lisa and Terry arrived home in Twin Mountains, she put Terry to bed first thing and then checked her mail. There was a letter addressed to her from a Lieutenant Colonel Jonathon Wright. She used a knife to open the envelope and sat quietly to read the letter.

June 10, 1950

Dear Miss Carter,

I'm not sure if you remember me or not. I was in Boston for a quick visit and attended a Boston Pops concert, a favorite of mine. I haven't seen you since we said good-bye at Pearl Harbor on the hospital ship. That night in Boston the piano player looked familiar to me. And when you played one of your solo selections, I knew that it was you.

Your playing is still a moving musical experience. Congratulations are in order. Now, the rest of the world can enjoy your special gift. I salute your accomplishments and am glad that you appear to be doing well. I wanted to stop by and say "hello," at the end of the concert, but duty called... I had a plane to catch and did not have time.

I remember that you had decided to carry your child. At the time, I was too involved with my own injuries to think about anything else. I want you to know how proud I was of you. I understood what a difficult decision you had to make. It was a privilege to escort you and your companions out of the Luzon jungle to civilization and freedom.

As for me, I've made a complete recovery from my wounds. I fanatically fought the advice of several doctors who wanted to amputate my leg. The Lord was with me. It finally healed and with therapy, I'm as strong as ever.

My mother and my daughter, Faith, accompanied me to the pops concert. She's been playing the piano since she was four, and she's now nine years old. She was mesmerized by your playing and remarked several times during the performance how powerful it was for her. Now, she's an enthusiastic fan of yours.

I'm currently attached to army intelligence based in Japan at MacArthur's headquarters. I had kept your old address and hope this note finds you well and happy. Again, congratulations.

Best Wishes
Jonathon Wright,
Lt. Col., USA

Chapter Thirteen

Tokyo, Japan — June 24, 1950

Lieutenant Colonel Jonathon Wright sat in the office of the Army Intelligence Evaluation Division, Tokyo, Japan, reviewing intelligent data from sources all over the world. He had read and reread the material in their files on the North Korean army. Something was up, but no one could connect the dots to predict what, when, or where. He wiped his eyes and leaned back in his chair. For hours he had tried to glean some clue that others had overlooked. His inability to predict explosive events angered him. He ceremoniously cleaned his pipe of cold ashes and filled it with Half and Half pipe tobacco. The first puff from a freshly lit pipe full of tobacco was always the best, and he closed his tired eyes to savor the moment.

Colonel Henry Lee walked into the office and took a seat at a desk facing Jonathon. Lee was an American-Japanese officer with a short compact build and a round face with laughing eyes. His good humor and mild disposition masked a very determined man who drove himself relentlessly. He was a graduate of the University of Hawaii with a degree in law. He and Jonathon had become close friends. Lee looked at the haggard lines around Jonathon's eyes and asked, "Any luck, Jon?"

"None, Colonel," Jonathon answered, carefully tamping his pipe so as to not let any of the live sparks land on his uniform. He already had several pairs of pants with burn holes. "Something is taking place, but I have to agree with the rest of you, I don't know what it is or if it's significant."

"Well, we can't produce miracles unless we have the information," sighed Lee, searching his briefcase for a notepad, which he dropped on his desk. "Do you remember the conversation we had a while ago about that prison commander on Luzon?"

Jonathon looked up at Lee, remembering how it had been five years ago. "Yes, he was a major, I believe. Like I told you, I hauled him off an American woman and forcibly restrained him. The women inmates eventually killed him. I can still see his eyes just before he died. His haunting look has stayed with me. I've often wondered what kind of person he was. Have you been able to locate any information about his family?"

"A couple of weeks ago, after our conversation, I started an investigation to determine what I could. Accurate Japanese military records are not easy to come by, but I've got something. The commandant was Major Toshio Taniguchi, a career army officer who did well in the pre-war Japanese army. He was a demanding officer with a long record of violence and brutality. He occasionally beat his subordinates inflicting permanent deformities on a few. In that respect he fit in well as one of the bright young officers."

"I can believe that of him," replied Jonathon, puffing his pipe.

"His father is Horio Taniguchi, a renowned violinist in Japan. His address is on this pad," said Lee, passing the notepad to Jonathon.

"Thanks, Colonel. I appreciate the information you've dug up. I wonder if I'm making a mistake opening a can of worms capable of inflicting more pain. Old wounds can still hurt, I know that from experience," mused Jonathon.

"That all depends on how badly you want to put that period of your life to rest, Jon. Since you're already in Japan, it might not hurt to pay the man a visit. The short bio sketches of him stated that he spoke some English and had visited the United States in the early thirties."

"You may be right, Colonel," replied Jonathon, taking the sheet of paper from the pad and placing it in his tunic pocket. "I'm going to turn in for the night. If I look at one more page, I'll scream. I'll see you in the morning, Colonel."

"Take care of yourself, Jon," said Lee again, looking at the weary lines under his eyes. "I wish we had more to offer General MacArthur on his daily briefing tomorrow. Why don't you take a couple of days off? You should have taken a longer leave last month. I don't know how you've been able to function as well as you have. If you need more time off just say the word."

"I appreciate your concern, Lee. It's friends like you that have helped a lot. I don't need more leave time just now, but a couple of days off would be fine," Jonathon replied, collecting his hat from the valet. "Good luck, Lee."

The air was warm and the skies above Tokyo were filled with stars glowing in the dark void. The half moon was hanging in the eastern sky on a base of cumulous clouds. Jonathon breathed easier. He was physically and emotionally exhausted. The officer's club stayed open twenty-four hours a day offering good food and drink. He entered the club and served himself a hearty breakfast of pancakes, sausage, and lots of coffee. He ate alone near a window watching the sun climb over the skeleton-like remains of bombed out buildings within the city.

Thoughts of his wife Hope and daughter Faith filled his heart and consciousness as soon as he left the intense atmosphere of the intelligence office. At work, he was able to apply himself to the task at hand. Once it was completed, his mind wandered to the loss he still mourned. Memories were priceless and painful. The club was beginning to fill with officers preparing for early posts. He saw an old friend of many years, Major Jim O'Hare, at the buffet line. Jim spotted him and took a seat at the table with his tray.

"You look beat, Jon," surmised Jim, a small wiry Irishman with flashing eyes. He went through life rarely taking anything too seriously, especially himself.

"It's been a rough night, Jim," conceded Jonathon.

"I'm glad I ran into you, Jon. I've got a staff conference in half an hour. After that I'll be on my way to the airport for a flight to Okinawa. I've got a parked Jeep outside. Would you turn it into motor pool for me?"

"Sure, I'll be glad to, Jim," answered Jonathon, suddenly smiling. "Lee just told me to take a few days off. How about if I take your Jeep for a couple of days? I've got a few errands to run in Tokyo."

"No problem. The Jeep is permanently assigned to my military police battalion. Use it as long as you want. I'll be in Okinawa several days. You could use some time. Your friends worry about you," Jim said sincerely. "The tank is full of fuel. Here are the keys."

"Thanks," said Jonathon, preparing to leave. "I'll see you around, Jim. Your Jeep has helped me make up my mind about something."

Jonathon left the club feeling better. He had decided to pay Mr. Taniguchi a visit! He drove through a main thoroughfare heading southwest out of the city. The picture-card panorama of Fujiyama rose from the relatively flat coastal plains to dominate the horizon. Solid and majestic Fujiyama loomed above the ash ruins of metropolitan Tokyo and its suburbs, like the fabulous Phoenix. Legend has it that the bird burns itself on a pyre of aromatic gum wood every five hundred years and rises from the ashes in renewed vigor and beauty.

Tokyo had been destroyed several times and always rose from the ruins in greater splendor. As early as 1923, earthquakes and fires destroyed the city killing over 150,000 people. Now the recently bombed ruins were well on their way to rising again. Jonathon marveled at the tenacity and industriousness of the people. New homes were being constructed and multilevel office buildings were beginning to dot the barren landscape of broken bricks and mortar.

Jonathon drove the Jeep to his quarters, where he showered and went to bed. He was exhausted. The minute his head touched the pillow his mind was filled with memories of Hope. Tears still came easy. Even now, five years after her violent death, he could hear her voice and knew that she was still with him. Her death in a train wreck had changed his life. More than ever he needed her soft and gentle presence. She was the inspiration and motivation for everything he did. Every memory, echoes from the past, she had called them, included Hope. Now, he was going through life like a lost soul without a rudder.

For a long time, he drank more than ever. It all started at Pearl Harbor during the final days of his physical therapy treatment involving his leg and arm injuries from the Philippines. Old friends were worried that his drinking would jeopardize his desire to stay in the army. One night after a heavy drinking session, he started a fight in the officer's club and had to be restrained by friends. Two days later he woke up in the navy hospital, where he had been treated for minor bruises from the brawl he had initiated. Deeply afraid of losing a way of life that he needed to cling to for his own sanity, Jonathon vowed to go on the wagon. For three years he had not touched a drop.

The devastating train wreck had taken place in Pennsylvania when Hope and Faith were traveling from Maine to California so that they could be with Jonathon while he was recuperating from his injuries. Hope was killed instantly when the passenger train was derailed.

Faith had only minor lacerations to her arm and back. Jonathon was unable to leave the hospital at that time, so his mother took Faith back to Monson so that she could continue in the same school system and keep her old friends, which became most important to her after the tragic loss of her mother. Just before the war started, Jonathon and Hope had moved into an apartment in Monson. They agreed that an apartment was more suited to their needs at that time. He had anticipated they would be together soon at the military installation he would be assigned to. The war came and destroyed all their plans, so Faith and Hope remained at the apartment in Monson.

Jonathon knew that it was not the best arrangement in the world for Faith, yet, he failed to do anything about it. Then came his period of drinking heavily. It helped him forget that he had a responsibility to his daughter. He went home to be with her as often as he could, and they had spent some good days together, but he always came away from the furloughs missing Hope more than ever. He considered resigning his commission and was assured by the army that as soon as his tour of duty in Japan was over, he would be transferred stateside to at least a two-year tour of duty at some New England university teaching in the Reserve Officer's Training Corps (ROTC). Jonathon and Faith both looked forward to that time when they could be together for an extended period as a family.

In every letter he received from Faith or his mother, Jonathon was informed of Faith's aptitude for music, and the piano especially. Jonathon insisted that she continue with her individual lessons on a regular basis. When he did make it home, he made it a point to take Faith out to musical shows, concerts, and other musical events. She was thrilled with their visit to the Boston Pops where Jonathon recognized Lisa.

Jonathon awoke midday from a restless sleep remembering that he had wheels in the form of the MP Jeep. An hour later, he was on the road heading southwest to the Tokyo address Lee had given him. It was several miles in the country far from the sprawling city limits. Miles of rice paddies and sugar cane fields dotted the area, taking up every square foot of land not used by roads or buildings. The land was intensely cultivated by the industrious farmers for maximum production of foodstuff for the large population.

Mr. Horio Taniguchi's address turned out to be a very modest home surrounded by tall trees and landscaped with hundreds of miniature pine trees in various sizes and shapes. Jonathon parked the Jeep off the street and removed the ignition key, unsure if he should continue, or if this was the right thing to do. His hesitancy had increased with every mile he drove. For some reason, he expected a different kind of home rather than the orderly and beautifully landscaped one before him. Ever since Lee had described the man to him his curiosity had been honed. Reluctantly, Jonathon followed the walkway as it meandered through a meticulously maintained garden. Admiring the beauty of the lush vegetation, Jonathon almost tripped over a man kneeling beside the pathway planting flowers.

"Oh, I'm sorry," exclaimed Jonathon. His knowledge of Japanese was very limited, so he did not even try to converse in the native language. He had knocked one of the plants out of the man's hand and exclaimed, "Did I hurt you?"

The Japanese man was slender of frame and build with a small mustache and white hair. He was dressed in a gray robe, a traditional Japanese garment, especially for home wear. The man did not speak until he stood in front of Jonathon and looked up at him. "No, you did not hurt me," the elderly man answered in English. "May I help you?"

Jonathon's mind frantically searched for the right words to announce his intentions. "I was distracted by the beauty of your garden and did not see you kneeling beside the path. I came to see a Mister Horio Taniguchi."

"I am Horio Taniguchi," he replied, observing the array of ribbons on Jonathon's uniform.

"Sir, I'm Lieutenant Colonel Jonathon Wright. I came to speak to you about your son, Major Toshio Taniguchi," Jonathon stated in a direct voice though he was a bundle of nerves. There was a reluctance on his part not to continue the conversation and he was frantically thinking of some way to gracefully leave the garden.

"Are you troubled by something, Colonel?" observed Mr. Taniguchi. "Would my son, by chance, be the source of your discontent? It is no secret that he has shamed our family and has been the source of much sorrow to his mother and myself. Please, come into my garden where we can share a cup of tea and discuss what is bothering you."

Jonathon was unprepared for such courteous and gracious informality. Part of the reason for the trip was to see what kind of man the cruel commandant had for a father. Jonathon had no guilt about being the instrument of his death, but he did have a lingering wonder if there might have been more to the man than he and the women prisoners had witnessed.

"I accept your offer of tea and hope that my visit does not rekindle hurtful memories," conceded Jonathon.

"How could such a conversation not be hurtful, Colonel?" Mr. Taniguchi gently placed the dropped flower in a vase of water and motioned for Jonathon to follow him. "Come, I have a pot of tea being kept hot on my brazier."

Jonathon followed the lively steps of the elderly gentleman as the narrow path wound around a small pool of water with a wooden veranda built over one edge of the pool. Overhead was a wooden arbor covered with wisteria vines. Lush purple blossoms hung from the arbor and lattice overhead. Around the edge of the pool, purple iris flowers were in full bloom. It was a beautiful secluded retreat where he felt at ease and surprisingly at peace. He had not anticipated this! The beauty and serenity of the setting was contrary to what he had expected to find. There was more to the frail elderly man pouring tea into two small cups, than he had imagined, although he was not sure what he did anticipate. The sharing of tea in a garden setting had spiritual connotations for the Japanese.

"I'm feeling your discomfort, Colonel Wright. Perhaps both of us need to talk openly so that we can put the past in order," stated Mr. Taniguchi, passing the tea cup to Jonathon with a respectful bow. "Were you present when my son was killed?"

Jonathon sat at the low table opposite Mr. Taniguchi, and accepted the tea with a bow. "Yes."

"Did you kill him?"

"I wounded him as he was assaulting a woman prisoner at the compound. His death came an hour later at the hands of the women inmates." Jonathon paused, uncertain if he should continue to be so graphic. Mr. Taniguchi's face was a study in stoicism, registering nothing Jonathon was able to discern. "I could have stopped the inmates, but I chose not to. I felt that justice had been well served by the deed. I saw a look on your son's face when the end was near, that has haunted me for the past five years. I know that he was a monster and that each of us must be responsible for the choices we make. What I'm trying to say and am probably doing it very badly, Mister Taniguchi, is that I saw, for a fraction of a second, a look of remorse and regret in your son's eyes. Was there more to the man that we did not see?"

"My son was a complex person, Colonel. Thank you for being honest and not judgmental. He was our only child and his mother and I worshipped him." Mr. Taniguchi slowly sipped his tea, and held his gaze at the pool of water as if he were studying his own reflection. "If you wish to understand my son, then you must first understand what Japan was like before the war."

"I'd like to hear what you have to say, sir."

With that, Mr. Taniguchi reviewed the recent history of Japan. The depression of the late 1920s and early thirties crippled the economic structure of many countries, including Japan and the United States. In Japan, the depressions fueled the rise of fanatical nationalistic militarism, which gained control of the government in the early thirties. Their expansion policies were responsible for World War II. The gains made in national wealth and culture over the past centuries were reversed and lost forever. Ultimately, all that remained of the Japanese state were the home islands. In 1937 war was declared against China. Four years later, war between the United States and Japan proved to be the final attempt in establishing a greater Asian conglomerate of nations. The militarists had gone too far and ended up destroying the nation they had pillaged and raped for fifteen years.

Jonathon listened in silence as the scholarly elder concluded his monologue by saying: "The United States was not Japan's greatest enemy. The fanatical militarists' takeover of Japan destroyed two hundred years of Japanese culture."

Chapter Fourteen

Mister Taniguchi continued with a sorrowful expression on his face. "My son was caught up in that movement and, like others, became intoxicated with the lust for power and domination. My wife and I had lost Toshio long before he died on Luzon. His mother was killed in a bomb raid early in 1945. Maybe we have a chance to find ourselves again. General MacArthur has done a magnificent job of building a foundation for that revolution to take place again."

Jonathon watched the tears form in Mister Taniguchi's eyes. Their eyes met for a second, then Mister Taniguchi quickly turned away and was silent for a long time. Jonathon felt like an intruder. "I'm sorry, sir. I did not mean to intrude."

"What did you expect, Colonel?" Mister Taniguchi questioned, wiping his eyes with the sleeve of his robe. "If I had the power, I would have prevented the outrages he committed, but his mother and I were helpless... Now she has gone and he has gone and I'm alone to bear witness to our failed attempts. I loved and respected Toshio's mother and am still mourning her loss. My son's death has been a source of pain greater than that for his mother because I'm partially responsible for the evil he perpetrated..."

"No, sir," cried Jonathon. "He bears that burden alone."

"A father does not pick and choose. By bringing Toshio into this world, I failed to indoctrinate him with the values his mother and I shared. That is our failure, not his. You claim that he raped an American woman under his care?"

"Yes, sir. I was a witness to that despicable deed. According to the inmates, it had become a daily routine after he took over the prison."

"Do you know the name of this woman prisoner?"

"Yes, sir," Jonathon answered.

Mister Taniguchi looked around at his garden. His eyes appeared to be half closed, and his facial features were strained. He began to breathe hard. "Would it be possible for me to apologize to the woman for the wrongs of my son?"

"I don't know, Mister Taniguchi," Jonathon replied nervously. He had not expected this turn of events. "I'm not at liberty to give you or anyone else her name. I witnessed her disgrace and cannot disclose her identity without her permission."

"I respect your position, Colonel. I'm familiar with the hatred for Japan that still exists in your country. We're trying to build a better Japan. In time prejudices may fade away and our two countries might become friends again."

"I'd like to think that it's possible, sir."

"I've been to the United States and was well treated. You are an industrious people much like the Japanese. Perhaps I might go to America one more time before I'm too old to atone for my son's sins. It's the least I should do," concluded Mister Taniguchi with a deep sigh.

Jonathon believed that the man was sincere in his desire to apologize for the atrocities of his son. "Sir, if you want, I promise to deliver any message you may wish to prepare for the American woman your son violated. There may be others that she would know of, and I'm certain she would pass on your message."

"Your offer can hardly be refused, Colonel. I'll need some time to prepare a statement to the woman."

"You may drop it off to me at my headquarters," suggested Jonathon, passing him his calling card. "If I'm not in, just have the duty officer place it in my mailbox."

"You're very kind, Colonel. I appreciate your generous offer. I will personally take it to your headquarters. Would you like more tea?"

"Thank you, sir." Jonathon was able to relax and let the solitude of the garden work its magic on him. They talked for an hour more about world events and personal things. Jonathon shared his grief of losing Hope with the kindly elder. By the time Jonathon left the garden, he had a warm feeling of affection for his dignified Japanese host.

Jonathon returned the borrowed Jeep to the motor pool and turned in for the night. The next morning he was rousted from a sound sleep by Colonel Lee, who had charged into his quarters announcing that the North Koreans had just invaded South Korea.

"My God," exclaimed Jonathon, jumping out of bed, dumbfounded at the unexpected news. "I'll be at HQ as soon as I can get dressed, Colonel."

Ten minutes later, he joined a conference at the Far East Command Headquarters. Colonel Lee was at the podium. "I'm glad you're here, Colonel Wright. Every officer with combat experience is desperately needed to command the units we're sending piecemeal into Korea. Your Ranger background makes you more valuable right now as a regimental commander than as an intelligence officer. The Army is scraping together every available man to form battalions into regiments. I'm placing you in command of an ad hoc regiment. You'll be assigned to regular army units already on the ground. Commandeer any equipment you need. Assemble Jeep radio crews capable of staying in touch with Eighth Army at Pusan. How soon can you leave, Jon?"

"Within two hours, sir," Jonathon answered. "What's the situation in Korea?"

"The North Koreans have crossed the thirty-eighth parallel with massive numbers of tanks and men. They're meeting light resistance. All we have in Korea are a few military advisers. Everything we have in Japan will soon be put into the fray. We've got to stop their advance. Any questions?"

"How will we get to Korea?" Jonathon asked.

"By plane. As soon as enough soldiers assemble to fill a plane, off they go. You'll have to sort them out once you get on the ground in Korea." Colonel Lee was asking a lot of Jonathon.

Jonathon swallowed hard at his new orders. His mind was running wild absorbing the responsibilities of commanding a regiment. He was going back into combat with a rag-tag group of men grown soft on occupational duty. "I don't like it, Colonel Lee, but I'll do my best."

Twenty-four hours later, Jonathon stepped off a DC-3 transport plane in Pusan, South Korea. He was met by an orderly for General Walker, commander of the Eighth Army and all US forces in Korea.

"I'm Captain Downs. General Walker asked me to meet you, Colonel Wright."

Jonathon, dressed in field clothes, was carrying a small duffel bag with personal gear, a thirty-caliber carbine over his shoulder and a forty-five-caliber pistol on his belt. "I'm glad to meet you, Captain." Jonathon returned the young Captain's salute and looked around the airfield. It was a beehive of activity.

"I have a Jeep just off the runway, Colonel Wright. There's been a change of plans. You've been assigned to a regiment on the line south of Seoul. Their commander and assistant commander have both been killed. Your job is to hold the main road link between Pusan and Seoul. We need time to build up our forces. You're part of that blocking force to buy us that time."

"Are things that grim?" asked Jonathon, following the Captain to the Jeep.

"Between you and me, it doesn't look good."

Jonathon was given a briefing on the current situation at Walker's HQ in Pusan. The North Koreans were smashing through every attempt by the South to block the roads. US troops were not doing much better. The North Koreans were using Russian tanks that were almost impossible to knock out with the light-weight rocket launchers then available to the Army. Artillery was almost non-existent. The order issued by Walker to US troops was to "hold at every cost." It sounded good in press releases, but to Jonathon it sent a chilling message that he and his men were expendable. Every career soldier understands that at some unexpected time he may find himself in that agonizing situation. It angered Jonathon because he had seen how ill-prepared the occupation troops were in Japan and no one listened. Now, they were paying a heavy price for indifference and lack of preparedness.

Jonathon was given command of the twenty-second regiment positioned south of Seoul. A helicopter was waiting for him. He climbed aboard without full knowledge of the chaotic conditions in Korea. Jonathon left without any situation report and without any specific orders except to delay enemy forces for as long as it was humanly possible to do the job. He interpreted the orders to mean stand until total destruction was imminent before giving ground to the enemy. On board the helicopter he met an old friend from the last war, Major Hal Jacobs. Jonathon embraced the muscular West Point graduate. The last time they had seen each other was on Luzon right after Jonathon was wounded.

"Where are you headed, Hal?" asked Jonathon, glad to see him.

"I'm your new executive officer, Colonel. I was surprised to see your name on the latest roster. How have you been? I heard about Hope. I'm sorry. I also heard rumors that you were thinking of retiring," replied Hal, hanging on to the safety straps.

"I gave it all up when I lost Hope, Hal. I almost lost my daughter too. I just wasn't ready to leave the army after Hope's death. It's been hard on Faith. Thankfully she's with my mother in Maine."

"Thank God there's someone waiting for you to come home to," Hal exclaimed. "You know we've been handed one hot potato don't you?"

"I've come to the same conclusion. We'll just have to do the best we can with what we've got. Rangers are used to accomplishing the impossible," answered Jonathon with a sly grin. "I'm really glad to have you with us, Hal. I feel better already about the task ahead."

The helicopter hovered directly above an open field at an elevation of two hundred feet. Small arms fire began hitting the aircraft. The pilot dropped behind a clump of pine trees landing with a heavy thud. Jonathon and Hal exited the craft and ran toward a Jeep pulled up just outside the rotors of the helicopter.

A nervous corporal motioned for them to get in the Jeep. "We're under attack."

"Where's the regimental command post?" Jonathon asked, gasping for breath as he and Hal climbed into the racing Jeep.

"We've been overrun, Colonel," replied the corporal, driving the Jeep at full speed along a cart track between two rice paddies. The smell was overpowering. "You get used to it after a while," noted the young driver.

The regiment was straddling a main road leading to Pusan. Two of its battalions had been decimated and were no longer viable fighting formations. Most of the officers had been killed. The third battalion was commanded by an inexperienced second lieutenant, fresh out of ROTC. Jonathon and Hal looked at each other in disbelief. The command post was a tarpaulin stretched between a half-track and several trees. A map was attached to one of the trees.

Jonathon glanced at the map to orient himself, but it didn't tell him anything. He asked the driver how the battalion was positioned along the road. The young corporal never had a chance to answer the question. A squad of North Korean soldiers had broken through the blocking battalion's line. The corporal was bayoneted. Jonathon killed three of the enemy with his carbine, driving the others to cover.

"My God," cried Jonathon. There was nothing he nor Hal could do except defend themselves against waves of North Korean soldiers that surrounded them. For two hours they held the hordes at bay until they ran out of ammunition. Jonathon slung the carbine over his shoulder and pulled his pistol. A North Korean soldier had managed to circle around them. He fired a full burst from his submachine gun at Jonathon. The force of the burst momentarily lifted him in the air before he collapsed on the ground.

Hal ran to the North Korean soldier, and with his bare hands, broke his neck. Then, he picked up the submachine gun and ran to Jonathon's side. For a moment the area was quiet. Suddenly the pulsating whir of helicopter blades could be heard. Hal looked up at the ungainly birds. The pilot was looking for a place to make a landing and hovered over a small section of a rice paddy. Hal picked up Jonathon and slung him over his shoulder and began a sprint to the helicopter. Enemy fire riddled Hal's body just as he dumped Jonathon on the floor of the helicopter. A soldier in the helicopter fired several bursts from his mounted machine gun, then stopped to drag Hal onto the floor, screaming for the pilot to lift off. The pilot pulled for full throttle as the craft shuddered from enemy fire. For what seemed an eternity, the aircraft vibrated violently and began to rise. The floor of the helicopter was covered with blood.

Chapter Fifteen

Three months later, Lisa moved to an apartment in Durham. She had been offered a job at the University of New Hampshire as a music instructor, after resigning her full-time position with the Boston Pops. The commute and expense back and forth from northern New Hampshire to Boston had taken too much of her time. Several of her acquaintances had formed a New Hampshire Symphony Orchestra with a base at the university. Lisa's acceptance of a position with the orchestra led to a salaried job at the university which paid more than her teaching job at Twin Mountains. The best part of the job was that she could take better care of Terry and spend more time with him. A normal life without long separations was something she looked forward to. Lisa was feeling good about the way her life was going.

Terry was already enrolled in the Durham kindergarten class. The days she could not be home after Terry completed classes, a next door neighbor looked after him. She had a daughter in the same class as Terry.

The first week of September had been hectic. Lisa had to prepare outlines for the three classes a week she had contracted for. She liked the academic atmosphere of the campus. The energy of the students was contagious. There was also a very serious down-to-earth demeanor among the older students, who made up sixty percent of the student body. They were World War II veterans taking advantage of one of the most generous pieces of legislature to come out of Washington — the G.I. Bill of Rights.

An education was made available to them, and the campuses of the nation were filled with mature men motivated and focused on obtaining an education. They introduced a more serious element to campus life overshadowing the excesses of the younger students. They had little time for frivolity or partying. The horrors of combat could be seen in the eyes of many of the veterans. The veterans gave a mature element of stability and purpose to the campus that would disappear soon after they graduated.

Lisa related to the veterans, for she too had experienced the war in a very unique way. Yet, she worried that the veterans on campus would be the most likely group to be critical of Terry. Consequently, she avoided taking him on campus because she did not want to subject him to an unpleasant incident with those men who might still harbor hatred for the Japanese. So far, she had not experienced any derogatory remarks. She frequently drew inquiring glances at grocery stores and other public places when Terry was with her, but many simply looked and wondered without passing judgment. She never explained his ancestry to strangers, and continued to keep her life as private as possible.

Lisa was content to stay at home with Terry when her work at the university and with the orchestra were completed. Occasionally she attended school functions, but felt uncomfortable and often out of place. She was beginning to get the reputation of a recluse.

The last Friday of the month Lisa returned mid-day to their apartment. Terry was still at school. She fixed a glass of lemonade and sat down at the kitchen counter when the phone rang.

"Hello," she answered.

"Is this Miss Lisa Carter?" asked a voice she did not recognize.

"Who's calling?" she asked, unwilling to give her name to a stranger.

"I'm sorry, this is Colonel Jonathon Wright," answered a weak-sounding voice.

"Now, I recognize your voice, Colonel. Yes, this is Lisa. How did you get my new phone number?"

"I called the Boston Pops business office for your number and address. I hope I'm not calling at a bad time." Jonathon's voice was barely audible.

"Of course not," she answered. "Are you all right, Colonel? I can barely hear you."

"Not really," he answered. "I've been assigned to the Portsmouth Naval Yard Hospital for recuperation and therapy. I was wounded in Korea the second day of the war. I've been in a lot of hospitals. They decided to send me to the hospital nearest to my home in Maine. I picked Portsmouth because when I get out I'm going to be assigned for a two-year tour of duty as commander of the ROTC unit in Durham."

"What a coincidence," remarked Lisa pleased to hear the news. "I just took a job here."

"I understand that. Listen, I'm not sure how long I'll be able to talk coherently. They just gave me a shot to ease the pain. Would it be possible for you to come down to the hospital? I have something I want to discuss with you, and I don't want to do it over the phone. I apologize if I sound mysterious, but you'll understand when I tell you."

"I could drop by later this afternoon or early evening," Lisa suggested, wondering what he wanted to talk about.

"Early evening will be fine with me. I'll be finished with my exercises by then. It'll be nice to see you again, Miss Carter."

"I'll be there by seven o'clock. If something comes up, do you have a number I can call?"

"Yes, it's room 88, phone number 92-W, and it's a direct line to my hospital bed. I hope I'm not interrupting any of your plans."

"Colonel Wright!" she scolded. "You're not interfering with anything. Rest well now, and I'll see you soon."

Jonathon answered with a thick tongue. "Thanks."

Lisa hung up the receiver and thought about the first time she had met the brave soldier. The feeling of giving up on life was something she would never forget. Thinking of it now was frightening, but back then, suicide looked like an easy way to eliminate the cruelties they had to endure. Then, out of the dark jungle a figure burst into the room while the Japanese commandant was violating her. The door broke in small pieces and the next thing she knew, the commandant was cringing on the floor, a pathetic human being. In that split second she no longer wanted to die, the world had changed!

The calm and gentle persuasion he brought to her in that room as he tried to comfort her, was an experience she had relived over and over. She and the other inmates were inspired by the Rangers. They not only saved lives, they gave new meaning to many who had lost the will to live. Lisa was one of the first to acknowledge that fact. She was anxious to bring Terry to see Jonathon. The Colonel's reaction was important to her.

Lisa waited at the driveway to her apartment for Terry's bus, visible in the distance. He and their neighbor's son, Ralph, stepped off the bus. Ralph was first. When he saw Lisa, he turned to look at Terry, who had been crying. His eyes were swollen and red. Terry saw his mother waiting and ran to her.

"What's the matter, Terry," she demanded, picking him up.

The young woman driver of the bus held the door open and stepped out to speak to Lisa. "Your son was sitting minding his own business when some of the older kids in the back began talking loud and hatefully about the Japanese. They messed up his hair and ripped his shirt before I noticed what was going on. I broke up the scuffle and have the names of the children involved," the driver handed a sheet of paper to Lisa. "I'm sorry this happened. I kicked the boys off the bus for a week. Your son has been a well-mannered little gentleman, and he did nothing to draw such behavior to himself."

"Thanks for letting me know," Lisa told the driver. "This is only his second week at a new school. I don't know what to do, but I'll do what I can to make sure there's no repeat performance."

"Good luck. If you need me for anything, give me a call."

"Thanks," Lisa replied.

The driver climbed back into the bus and drove off.

Lisa turned to Terry. "Did you hear the driver?"

"Yes," he answered, waving bye to Ralph.

"Did you see it, Ralph?" Lisa asked.

"Those older guys just kept calling him names like Tojo and hari-kari," answered Ralph. "We were sitting together and they kept cuffing him on the head. I was scared they would hurt me too."

"Well, we'll see that they don't do that again. Thanks for being a friend to Terry. Now you better run along so that your mother won't worry about you."

"See you Monday, Terry," hollered Ralph, running home.

Lisa took Terry's hand and walked slowly into the apartment. This was the first incident where another person had made racial slurs to his face. Lisa was furious that it had happened so early in the school year when he was alone in a completely strange environment. She had prayed that it would be a positive time in his young life. Lisa looked down at him and her heart beat faster. She loved him with all the love a mother was capable of having.

Terry was a quiet child that any mother would be proud of. He was like a small adult in many ways. He walked into

135

the house beside his mother still holding her hand. There was a determined look on his face that made her want to cry. It wasn't defiance, but it reflected an inner strength that the five-year-old was going to make the best of an uncomfortable situation. He was not afraid. What bothered him the most was that his friends on the bus had seen him crying. It was his first encounter with racism and Lisa was concerned, yet, there was an element of relief that the inevitable meeting had taken place. She was encouraged with the way Terry had handled the situation.

As soon as they got in the house, Lisa called the numbers the bus driver had given to her. There were three boys. Two were brothers and the third was a neighbor further down the road. Lisa called the home of the two boys, Larry and Thomas Holmes.

Mrs. Holmes answered. "Hello."

"Hello. This is Lisa Carter. Are you the mother of Larry and Thomas Holmes?"

"Yes, is anything wrong?" asked Mrs. Holmes, detecting a determined tone in Lisa's voice.

"That all depends on how one looks at it," claimed Lisa, proceeding to tell her what had taken place on the bus. "Before I continue, I want to know what you plan to do about it. The bus driver witnessed most of the episode."

"Was your son hurt?"

"Not physically, but who knows what such behavior has on a five-year-old? My son Terry, is a Japanese-American, and I'm not going to stand by and have him accosted and insulted by older boys who should know better," promised Lisa, trying to control her anger. Normally she was very much in control of her emotions, but the thought of someone taking advantage of her son unleashed a powerful urge to seek justice.

Mrs. Holmes detected the rage and offered an apology for her son's behavior. "I can assure you that your son will never be treated that way by my boys again. Give me a half hour, Mrs. Carter, and I'll be there at your place with the boys. I'd say that the first order of business is an apology to you and your son."

"I couldn't agree more, Mrs. Holmes. Thank you for being so fair-minded," Lisa replied, breathing easier.

"Thank you for bringing it to my attention."

True to her word, Mrs. Holmes pulled into the driveway with the two boys. She made them walk up the stairs to the porch in front of her and ring the doorbell.

Lisa saw the two boys on the porch. They were not very happy. She opened the door. "Hello, I'm Terry's mother."

"My brother and I came by to say that we're sorry about the things we said and did to Terry," the older boy volunteered.

"I believe that you should say that to Terry instead of to me," she said, motioning them into the living room where Terry was sitting on the couch. He was shy and uncomfortable. "Terry, these two boys have something to say to you."

He stood up and looked down at the floor for a moment, then he confronted the two boys.

"Terry," began the older boy. "Me and my brother Tom apologize for the way we acted. My mother suggested that we should shake hands and put it behind us."

Larry extended his hand to Terry who was anxious to shake. Thomas also stepped forward. "That goes for me too. We were wrong to say those things to you."

Terry took his hand and asked eagerly, "Does that mean we can be friends?"

"Sure, if you want," replied Larry with a grin. "My dad was a soldier and he told us that the most courageous soldiers in the army were the Japanese-Americans fighting in Italy. We didn't really mean what we said. We thought that it would make us look big to our friends, but we were wrong."

Lisa and Mrs. Holmes smiled at each other, pleased with the outcome. A lesson in tolerance and humility had just been learned.

"I want to thank you boys for coming by," said Lisa, turning to Terry. "Is there something you want to say, Son?"

"No... except thanks for letting me be your friend," replied Terry, beaming all over. To be accepted by older boys as a friend was a treat for a five-year-old.

"Later this fall after the leaves have fallen, maybe I could hire you boys to do some raking for me. I'll pay the going rates in the neighborhood," suggested Lisa. The boys eagerly looked up at their mother.

"The boys would be pleased at a chance to earn some extra money," Mrs. Holmes answered for them. "We must be going now. I have a roast in the oven."

Terry and his mother stood on the porch watching the boys get back into their mother's Ford. Mrs. Holmes had given Lisa a hug before leaving. Terry waved from the porch as they drove down the street. Lisa was satisfied with the way Mrs. Holmes handled the situation, and Terry was pleased about the prospect of having older boys as friends. They were settling into the neighborhood on a positive note!

Lisa combed Terry's black hair away from his eyes with her index finger. "You know son, as you grow older, you'll find that people who say bad things about others really don't like themselves. We feel good when others like us, but it's just as important that we like ourselves. The things bad people say should not change that. Most people accept little boys like you when you're kind, respectful, and polite to others. If you listen to the little voice inside of you and act upon it, you'll seldom be wrong."

Terry did not understand all that his mother told him, but he knew that she loved him. "My teacher seems to like me."

"Of course she does. Now, what do you say if we have a quick bite to eat. Afterwards, we can take a ride to a place where they make submarines. Go wash your hands and I'll make some sandwiches."

"Mom," he asked, stopping at the screen door. "Do they make toy submarines or real ones?"

"Real big ones, Son," she smiled.

An hour later, they left the house. Lisa was more quiet than usual. Two things weighed heavily on her mind. The first was Jonathon's reaction to Terry. She had never mentioned him to Jonathon. Since she left the prison camp, most of her conversations were limited to their time on the hospital ship from Guam to Pearl Harbor. They had exchanged a few letters before the war ended, but not a word in the past five years. His unusual request for her to visit him had to be for something out of the ordinary. Jonathon Wright was not an impulsive person who would do rash things on a whim. She had detected a hesitancy on his part. The more she thought about it, the more she worried that it might have been better to have left Terry behind.

Lisa drove the Studebaker to the visitor center at the main gate of the navy yard. Two gray submarines were sitting in the water beside the center. Terry was fascinated by the ships. Workmen were moving about on the deck and a large crane was lifting pieces of equipment through an opening on the top deck.

"You stay in the car and watch the boat, Terry. I'll be right back. Do you understand?" she insisted firmly.

Terry knew that when she used that tone of voice, she really meant what she said. "I will, Mom. Is that a real gun on the boat?" he asked pointing to the deck gun.

"Yes, Terry," she replied, locking the Studebaker.

A few minutes later she returned with two visitor passes. She pinned one on Terry and clipped one on her blazer pocket and started the car. A marine sergeant at the gate stopped her.

"I have two passes to the hospital, sergeant," she pointed to the passes. "How do I get there?"

"Just follow the blue 'H' signs ma'am. They'll lead you to the left after the bridge. It's just a few hundred yards. Enjoy your stay."

Lisa drove over the narrow bridge following the signs and stopped in a parking lot for the hospital. "Come, Terry, Mom is going to meet an old friend, a soldier that has been wounded. He's inside expecting us. I want you to stay close to me. Don't be frightened of the sick and wounded men we may see."

As soon as they stepped into the receiving area, Terry looked up at her and said, "It smells like medicine in here, Mom."

"Yes, it does, but we must be quiet so that we don't disturb those who are trying to sleep." Lisa held his hand and stopped at the main desk. "I'm here to see Colonel Jonathon Wright."

"Let's see," answered a pharmacist mate, running his finger through a roster list of patients. "Oh, yes. He's our only army patient. We're honored to have a Medal of Honor recipient. You'll find his room down the corridor, 112. Normally we would not permit children under ten, but since the Colonel is in a private room, I don't see anything wrong in letting the boy visit. They've just finished serving dinner. Enjoy your visit Ma'am. By the way, I need your name for the records."

"I'm Lisa Carter and this is my son, Terry. Thank you for making an exception with Terry."

"You're welcome, Mrs. Carter."

Lisa continued to hold Terry's hand and slowly walked down the corridor checking numbers. The door for room number 112 was open. She could see a patient sitting in bed looking out the window. His upper torso was sheathed in plaster with his right arm in a sling. She stared at his left sleeve. It was empty!

Chapter Sixteen

Lisa was startled by the discovery and involuntarily held her breath. Jonathon heard her and turned his head. She saw sadness and loneliness in his face. He recognized her, and smiled. "It's nice to see you again, Lisa. I was afraid you might not make it today."

"What else would an old friend do, Colonel?" she insisted. "This little boy with me is my son, Terry. Terry, this is Colonel Wright, a very brave soldier and a good friend of mine."

"I'm glad to meet you, Terry. You'll have to excuse my unsightly appearance. I'd shake hands with you if I could, but I can't. A lot of my friends have autographed the cast I'm wearing. Would you like to sign your name on it?"

Terry looked at the man wrapped in white bandages. At his young age Terry did not completely understand the severity of Jonathon's injuries, but he was mature enough to know that the soldier had been badly hurt. "Yes, I can print my name," he answered proudly.

"He's a quick learner for a five-year-old," added Lisa, taking a pen from her blazer pocket. "Here I'll hold you so that you can put your name on Colonel Wright's arm cast."

"If you place your name on the cast, that means we're friends. What do you think about that, Terry?"

"I think it will be swell," he replied, carefully printing his name on the white plaster cast. When he was focused on doing something, he had a habit of holding his tongue between his lips. After he was done, he looked at the other names on the cast. "Are you going to sign it, Mom?"

"If the colonel doesn't mind, I will." Lisa placed Terry back on the floor.

"First of all, the colonel has a name, Jonathon. I like it when my friends call me Jon. Second, I'd be honored to have you sign my cast, Lisa Carter."

Lisa opened the pen and signed her name below Terry's. Her glance wandered to the empty left sleeve. It touched her not because it was offensive to her, but, because Jonathon did not deserve to be so grievously wounded.

Two nurses entered the room. One administered medication to a bottle with a tube feeding into his right shoulder. The other nurse gave him two pills by his mouth and held a glass of water with a straw for him to drink. When they left he laid his head back against the pillows and looked at Lisa. He smiled for a second, embarrassed that she was seeing him in this condition.

"I have to be fed every meal," he confessed in a low voice. "You look good, Lisa. I remember how you looked when Faith and I saw you in Boston... You must be wondering why I asked you to come. Please, pull up a chair where I can see both of you. I get tired when I talk too much, so bear with me."

Lisa did as he asked and directed Terry to sit beside her. "You don't have to apologize, especially to me, Jon."

"You'll find an envelope in the stand beside my bed. The letter was addressed to me at my Tokyo address. I received it a long time after I left Japan. The mail followed me from Pearl Harbor, to San Francisco, to Portsmouth. Inside, you'll find another envelope addressed: To Whom It May Concern. Please, open that letter and read it. I've agonized over the decision to let you see it. I know how difficult some things have been for you. Perhaps this letter will discuss things that you just as soon not know, but how will you be certain if you don't read it? Remember, I am only the messenger, and I have been that because I believe you may find some answers to the questions you've been searching for. If the letter hurts, I'm so sorry, and apologize. I've done this thing praying that it might bring you some peace, Lisa. I'm the last person in the world to want to hurt you."

"I believe you, Jon," answered Lisa, fingering the inner letter.

"If you want to be private, Lisa, you may go into a lounge across from my door, it'll give Terry and I a chance to get better acquainted. I believe you'll find the letter self-explanatory."

"If you don't mind," Lisa answered, looking at Terry. "Mommie will be right back. You can tell Colonel Wright all about your new school in Durham."

Lisa exited the room with a lump in her throat and quickly entered the lounge. She devoured the contents of the letter holding her breath in anticipation:

Tokyo, Japan

June 25, 1950

To Whom It May Concern;

Yesterday I was paid a visit by a remarkable young soldier, Lieutenant Colonel Jonathon Wright. We talked of many things and shared tea in my garden. He was troubled about the death of my son, Toshio, the prison camp commandant. Colonel Wright did not apologize for being the instrument of death, indeed he believed that justice was well served. Yet, the death troubled him because of the sadistic behavior of my son and the men under his command.

I am Toshio's father and bear some responsibility for his actions. His barbaric behavior was contrary to every value his mother and I have embraced. He violated every virtue and standard of behavior that guides civilized man. I am sorry for that conduct and if it was in my power, I would erase the sordid acts and replace them with the healing grace of kindness and compassion which transcends every race and culture.

Five years have passed since the war ended and I have agonized every day over the death of my son. It would have been easier to bear if he had been a brave soldier defending his country. Death would have had meaning and we could honor his courage and sacrifice… Alas, that honor has been denied his aging father. Instead of honor, I hang my head in shame and regret that he was my son. At least his mother has not had to bear the shame. She died in one of the bombing raids and never knew the truth.

If he had lived, and I was to learn of his behavior, the justice which Colonel Wright mentioned would not have been carried out by strangers. I personally would have been the instrument of death.

Across the miles of a mighty ocean, I send you my apologies, and extend a hand in friendship. It is right and proper to detest Toshio's actions, but, I beg of you, do not extend that hatred to all of the Japanese people.

I believe Colonel Wright will deliver this letter to you as he promised. I hope that you derive some measure of peace and consolation from my message. May God be with you.

Toshio's Father

She read the letter with tears gathering in her eyes blotting out the pages. Quiet sobs filled the empty lounge. Sitting rigidly on the edge of a chair, Lisa cleared the tears with a handkerchief and went over the letter again, word for word. It did not anger her, instead, it comforted her that someone else in the world was sharing her sorrow. She was encouraged by its sincere, uplifting tone in perfect English. Now, she understood why Jon requested a visit in person. The news he had to share was a heartfelt message from a tormented father. She had empathy for the gentleman.

Several visitors entered the lounge and sat down. Lisa excused herself and went into a women's restroom off the lounge and splattered water on her face. She did not want Terry to see that she had been crying. Lisa looked at herself in the mirror. Her thick auburn hair framed her small face. Earrings with an American flag dangling from a gold chain hung from her ear lobes. She thought she looked pale and squeezed her cheeks just before she darted back to Jonathon's room.

Terry was standing at the window describing to Jonathon what he saw on the partially submerged submarine next to the hospital. He turned to look at his mother and ran into her waiting arms. He saw that she had been crying. "Why are you crying, Mom?"

"I'm all right, Terry," she reached to pick him up and sat down on the chair with him on her lap. "You know how easy it is for Mom to cry when I'm happy and excited."

Jonathon observed her closely as she embraced Terry, hoping that he had not made a mistake. The letter had to have been a powerful message from out of nowhere.

Lisa replaced the letter in the drawer. "It was certainly not what I expected," she told him in a low voice. "The fact that you approached the man is not a surprise to me, Jon. I believe I would have done the same thing if I had been in your shoes. Thank you for being the messenger. Friends are a rare gift in this world."

"I'm relieved, Lisa. I've been uncertain about it for a long time."

"How did you perceive the man?" she inquired.

"I was surprised. He was not the person I expected to find. He's a well-educated man who speaks excellent English. I had a hunch that he was an honest man tormented by memories of his son's acts of cruelty. I spent a couple of hours with him and came away thinking that I had just been in the company of a fine human being. Sounds strange doesn't it?"

"Not really, considering what's taking place in the world today. One day a country is a friend and the next day it's an enemy. Will you ever see him again?"

"I doubt it," Jon replied. "Under normal circumstances, with an arm missing, I'd be discharged from the army. They're making an exception in my case at the University of New Hampshire. As soon as I'm fitted with my artificial arm, I'm going to command the ROTC unit at the university for a tour of two years. So my travels to Japan are finished. Would you like to meet him?"

"I'm not sure. I've got to think about it," mused Lisa. "Little Terry is too young to understand all the innuendoes taking place around him right now. Perhaps I could write a reply...." Lisa saw the deep lines around Jon's eyes. He looked exhausted. "All we've been talking about is me. How about you? I sympathize with what your injuries have done to your army career. Sometimes I get wrapped up in my own worries without thinking of others. Is there anything I can do for you?"

"Whenever you might have the time, a familiar face is always nice to see," Jonathon suggested.

"I'd like that. It's a short drive down from Durham. Has your wife been to see you?" she asked.

"No, my wife, Hope, was killed in a train crash several years ago. I thought you knew. My mother and Faith, my daughter, are coming for a visit at the end of the week. If you could make it then you could meet them," suggested Jon. The pain killers were taking affect. He was getting drowsy.

Lisa felt stupid asking the question. For a man who does nothing but give of himself, he certainly has had his share of traumatic experiences. Her problems seem small by comparison.

"You're looking tired, Jon. Terry and I'll be leaving. Thanks for being such a good friend. Get well soon." Lisa bent over him and gently kissed him on the forehead. "Sleep well Jon, sleep well."

The sight of Jon covered with bandages and casts bothered her. She had been with wounded soldiers for several weeks before the war ended, and she was shipped out of the Pearl Harbor Hospital. Instead of being places of gloom and discouragement, they frequently were havens of hope and belief in a better future. Her spirits had been lifted by the support of one another in the wards. The most seriously wounded were given the most support of all. The other soldiers and sailors circled the wagons around those most in need. No one suffered alone unless it was by request.

Memories of Jonathon, when he led the raid on the prison compound, contrasted with the soldier she saw at the Navy Yard. On Luzon he had projected an air of tireless invincibility as did his fellow Rangers. Fearless and courageous in combat, they were models of compassion and sensitivity to the women inmates. She would always remember that part of Jonathon. She attributed her physical and emotional survival to the gentle decency he displayed to her in the first two minutes they met in the bedroom of the commandant's house.

Lisa checked Terry lying on the seat beside her. It had been a long day. She smiled at the way he could sleep so completely with every muscle in his tiny body relaxed. Jon didn't say a word about Terry's ancestry, and she was not sure how she should take that. One of the reasons she was so glad to see him was the chance to show Terry. His reaction to her son was important to her, yet, in that respect, the visit had yielded nothing! Jon's apparent acceptance of Terry could have been a manifestation of his inherent decency and courtesy. Even if he had disapproved, he would not tell her so!

Friday afternoon turned out to be warm and sunny. The campus was filled with students sitting under the trees on the well-maintained lawns. Lisa left the university in a good mood, looking forward to meeting Jon's mother and daughter. Lisa and Terry entered the Portsmouth Navy Yard at about four in the afternoon with increasing anxieties and a tinge of paranoia that had become a permanent part of her psyche since Terry was born. Just how Jon's mother and daughter would react held her in nervous anticipation.

The duty nurse at the desk told Lisa that Jonathon had two visitors and was on the terrace overlooking the river. They were directed to the terrace where they found Jonathon propped up in a sitting position in his hospital bed. An elderly woman was bent over him. A young girl of about ten years was watching the boats travel the river.

Jonathon looked much more alert than he had been on her previous visit. He recognized Lisa and Terry from the corner of his eye as soon as they walked through the large French doors. "Ah, here comes an old friend, Ma."

Lisa was relieved that he had much better color today. "Hello, Colonel," She greeted him warmly.

The woman turned to Lisa. "Ma, I want you to meet Miss Lisa Carter and her son, Terry. Lisa, this is my mother, Lillian Wright, and the young lady hanging on the balcony is my daughter, Faith."

Mrs. Wright extended a hand to Lisa. "It's nice to meet you, Lisa. My son was just telling me that you stopped by this week. I was hoping I'd have a chance to meet you. We just came down from Monson, Maine. It's about a four-hour drive. It's nice that you come to visit Jon."

"I'm pleased to meet you, Mrs. Wright," Lisa replied, grasping her hand with both of hers. The naturalness of their meeting allowed Lisa to breathe easier.

"Come here, Faith," Mrs. Wright motioned to her granddaughter. "Say hello to Miss Carter and little Terry."

Faith was an active child with dark brown hair and inquisitive brown eyes. She smiled and seemed happy to meet Lisa. At first she looked at Lisa and then at Terry with a curiosity she did not try to hide. There was no animosity or shock, only inquisitiveness. Lisa liked her the minute she saw her. There was a modest, almost shy, demeanor about her that was cute and becoming. "I'm glad to meet you, Faith."

"I remember you," she remarked, filled with excitement. "Daddy and I went to the Boston Pops one day and you were playing the piano. You were wonderful. Daddy told me that he knew you. I'm taking lessons on the piano."

"Why thank you, Faith. I'm glad you liked it. Music has been an important part of my life. Continue with your lessons; music has a way of enriching our lives. I hope Terry is attracted to it, but he's a little young now. Your daddy has told me about you."

"I like music but I couldn't carry a tune in a wheelbarrow," Jonathon smiled.

"You take after your father, Jon," added Mrs. Wright. "I've been worried about you. When he's overseas I'm afraid to answer the phone or open mail from the department of the army for fear that it's bad news."

"Ma," protested Jonathon. "I would have gone crazy if I did not have the Army to occupy my time. I love the Army and am proud to be a part of it. I know it has been rough on you and Faith, like it was on Hope. I'll be happy when I can get out of this bed to start my new post at the university."

"I just started a new job at the university," Lisa mentioned. "So far, I like it fine. It gives me a chance to work with the new symphony orchestra being organized. That's been exciting. It'll be nice having you on campus, Jon."

"What about the Boston Pops?" he asked.

"I was hesitant to give up my position there, but I could not continue traveling back and forth. It was a wonderful experience and, occasionally, I'll go back for special performances."

"How long will it be before they fit you with your new arm?" asked Mrs. Wright, turning to Jonathon.

"They're working on it now, Ma. I hope to start work before the end of second semester. My arm probably won't be ready by then but that won't prevent me from functioning in the classroom."

They were interrupted by an orderly delivering Jon's supper. Mrs. Wright suggested that while he was eating, the four of them could get something to eat at the hospital cafeteria. Jon had requested that because he did not want them to see him being spoon fed like a baby.

Before she left for the cafeteria, Lisa placed an envelope on his food tray. He was surprised and looked into her eyes.

Lisa explained in a low voice. "This is an answer to the letter you brought me. I'd like to share it with you. I don't know the man's name or address. Would you see that he gets it?"

"You know I will," Jon assured her. "Are you sure you want me to read it?"

"It's important that I share it with you," she answered with a wry smile. Lisa patted the cast on his right arm and left to catch up with Mrs. Wright waiting at the door.

Jon had the orderly open the letter for him before touching his supper.

An answer from, To Whom It May Concern;

Colonel Wright gave me the letter you wrote. He has proven to be a good friend. I do not know your name and he did not offer it. My immediate reaction to the letter is relief that the suffering and agony caused by your son has been partially mitigated. I thought that I was alone in my despair and anger.

No one can undo what has been done. It was an experience that is impossible to forget, but I can assure you that I have tried to not let the incident destroy my life. The truth is, I cannot ever forgive your son, and you should know that I in no way whatsoever, hold you responsible. Your son made the choice and paid the consequences. I understand and welcome your compassion, but it is unfair for a father to be blamed for the deeds of an offspring.

I have news that may surprise you. Your son impregnated me. Nine months later, I gave birth to a baby boy. He's now five and a half years old and has started the first grade. He's alert and intelligent and I love him dearly. His Japanese ancestry is evident. I can share with you the fact that I agonized over the decision to have an abortion. After carefully examining the alternatives, and the accompanying ramifications, I decided to have the baby and have not regretted the decision.

Across the miles I say thank you for the kindness of writing. Sharing your feelings with me has helped more than you'll ever know. Again, thank you.

Sincerely, Madame X

Chapter Seventeen

Later that evening, Lisa invited Mrs. Wright and Faith to return to Durham with her and Terry, to stay for the night. Lisa promised to bring them back to Portsmouth first thing in the morning. She had planned to take Terry to the Nubble Lighthouse in York, Maine, and it was on her way. Lisa was pleased that her offer was accepted.

Jonathon's mother looked tired. Terry was traditionally in bed by eight o'clock. As soon as they got to the apartment Lisa put him to bed even though it was earlier than usual. Within seconds he was sound asleep. Faith had solicited a promise from Lisa to play the piano before bedtime. Lisa closed Terry's bedroom door and walked to the piano in the living room.

"Do you have any favorites?" Lisa asked.

Faith was excited. "Oh, I love *Canadian Sunset, Mona Lisa, Bali Ha'i,* and *Some Enchanted Evening.*"

"Those are good ones, Faith," Lisa said, turning on the bench. She played softly so as to not wake Terry, even though it was her style to not hammer the keys. No matter what songs she played there was a soothing quality to her technique. It was impossible to listen to Lisa's playing and not get caught up in the feelings the music portrayed. She did long medleys of the ones Faith mentioned and several of her favorite ballads, such as *Bouquet of Roses,* as sung by a popular country artist, Eddy Arnold. "I like his style of singing and the way he seems to feel the songs he selects. Some of the country music is beautiful in its plaintive, simple style."

"You like most kinds of music then," surmised Mrs. Wright, sitting comfortably on the couch.

"Oh yes, there's beauty in all forms of music. A person's taste may favor one style over another but the universality of music is that all of it has the ability to touch our hearts." Lisa turned her back to the piano. "My guest room is always available to you, anytime you come to visit Jonathon. What do you say if I fix us a cup of hot cocoa. I find it relaxing before bedtime."

"That would be nice, Lisa." Mrs. Wright smiled in agreement. "I didn't expect to be so tired. I've been worried sick about Jon. I'm so glad that he has a friend close by. He needs friends even though he doesn't know it."

"Come on into the kitchen while I put some water on to heat." Lisa motioned them to the small table beside a window looking out on the porch.

"Kitchens seem to be the place where everyone is the most comfortable," Mrs. Wright said, noting the orderliness of the room. "You do a great job of keeping things neat and clean, Lisa."

"Our kitchen at home was the favorite room, too," Lisa replied. "I suppose it stems from the tradition of breaking bread in fellowship."

Lisa warmed several cinnamon rolls and served them with the cocoa. The three gathered around the table and became better acquainted with each other. Mrs. Wright was especially impressed with Lisa's casual graciousness. She had a gift of being herself without pretense. Shortly after drinking her cocoa and eating one of the delicious buns, Faith volunteered to go to bed. The guest room had twin beds. Lisa showed them the bathroom and where she stored the towels and linen. Lisa and Mrs. Wright returned to the kitchen for a second cup of cocoa.

"Please feel free to retire whenever you want, Mrs. Wright. Traveling and visiting can be exhausting. I saw Jon a week ago. He was much improved today, his color was natural and he seemed to be more responsive. You and Faith seemed to buoy his spirits. I thought that he was very positive about his new assignment at the university."

Jonathon's mother sighed. Lisa saw despair on her face and was concerned. "Jonathon has been a lost soul since the death of Hope. A part of him died with her. I still worry about him. I know that he was drinking heavily for a while. That was out of character for him. He rarely drank except socially. It wasn't the alcohol so much as it was his attitude. He just didn't seem to care about anything. I hope you don't mind me sharing these things with you," said Mrs. Wright.

Lisa held her hands. "Of course not, Mrs. Wright. I don't know Jon that well, but I can tell you that he's a son you have every right to be proud of. I'll always be his friend. He saved my life and the lives of my friends and companions from a ghastly death in the prison camp. If there is anything I can do to repay that debt, I will do it with pleasure."

"He doesn't talk much about his war experiences. I didn't even know about his Medal of Honor until one of his friends told me. Faith has been most anxious to see him. I warned her about his arm. She's a very mature child for her age, but she's worried that she's losing him. He hasn't been forthcoming in his responsibility to Faith, and that still worries me," Mrs. Wright confided in Lisa.

"Jon told me that the move to New Hampshire will give him a chance to be a father to Faith," Lisa shared her conversation. "I felt that he was sincere and was anxiously looking forward to it. She's lucky to have you, Mrs. Wright. Losing a mother at such a young age must be horrifying. I can't imagine what she must be going through."

"Sometimes she withdraws into her music. She's been taking lessons for five years and is doing quite well. I haven't known how to handle her, because she has picked up on the fact that her father doesn't want to care for her," continued

Mrs. Wright, relieved to be able to talk about personal feelings with Lisa. "I can't say that it's rejection. I believe that Faith reminds Jon of the fact that Hope is gone, and I don't know how to explain that to her. She idolizes her father. You're a very kind person, Lisa. The minute you came onto the terrace today, Jon perked up. It was instantly noticeable. I thank you for that."

"When will you be going back to Maine?"

"I had planned to return home Saturday evening," replied Mrs. Wright.

"You're welcome to stay as long as you like."

"I appreciate your offer. I'm so glad Faith and I were able to meet you. Now, if you don't mind, I'm going to turn in. It's been a long day. You've been a most gracious host Lisa, goodnight."

"Goodnight, Mrs. Wright, rest well." Lisa showed her the bathroom and bedroom light switches and returned to the kitchen to clean up the table.

Unable to sleep, Lisa walked out onto the porch to sit quietly in the cool September air. The moon sat squarely on top of the crown of a large sugar maple tree on the lawn. Fall is her favorite time of year. The death of summer evokes a melancholic response. She thought of snow-capped peaks and whispering canyons and memories of her childhood in the majesty of the White Mountains. On evenings like this, when the earth was embraced in the solitude of the night, the silence could be overpowering.

"Solitude of the night," she whispered softly, staring into the dark voids of the sky. At times like this she felt alone, insignificant, and unfulfilled. Memories of Jeff were never far from her mind. His swift rejection of her at the end of the war still hurt, because it was based on his hatred of Terry and all that he represented. She struggled with his denial of support when she needed it the most. If he had truly loved her, as he had proclaimed, then he could have adjusted somehow to Terry's right to live.

Jeff had telephoned Lisa a couple of years after the war to tell her that he was moving to California and was engaged to marry. He never mentioned one word about Terry or asked how she was doing. She had sarcastically wished him well, and true to her disposition, suffered his insensitivity in silence and lived with the hurt. She had placed all of her hopes and dreams for the future in Jeff, and he had gone his separate way without a word or thought of the turmoil it created for her. She had cried for hours.

The first two or three years after Terry was born were difficult. She worked hard to maintain a normal home environment for Terry and herself. Being a single parent in puritanical New Hampshire was not the easiest thing to do, but she did it by holding her head high and never answering the gossip mongers that live in every small town. There had been a few men who expressed interest in her, one was a trombone player in the Boston Pops Orchestra. She liked him and they dated a few times. As soon as he discovered that she had a child, he fell all over himself trying to get away. She never told him how she got pregnant. They haven't spoken a word since.

Lisa was thirty-one years old and had resolved herself to the fact that having a son would turn most any normal suitor away. It made her love and protect Terry more than ever.

The next morning, Lisa insisted on preparing pancakes for everyone. They ate together around the kitchen table. Lisa felt good about that, it made her apartment seem more like a home. When they were finished, Faith asked Lisa to play two of her favorite songs, *Mona Lisa* and *Bali Ha'i*. Lisa sat at the piano and played the two songs. Faith watched every movement of her hands.

When she was finished, Lisa asked Faith a question. "This old piano was here in the apartment when I moved in. A couple of the keys are off. Can you tell me which ones?"

Faith smiled at the question and sat on the stool Lisa vacated, running through the scale. "I could be wrong, but I think G and B are flat," she answered.

"That's correct, Faith," exclaimed Lisa. "You've developed a fine ear for such a young pupil. Your grandmother and father should be proud of you."

"We certainly are, Lisa," admitted Mrs. Wright. "You have a unique style on the keyboard that is most pleasing to the ear. I played for years but arthritis curtailed my playing long ago."

"I'm sorry to hear that," Lisa said. "Your son will be expecting you. I'm ready to leave if you are."

"Thank you for making this trip so much easier for me," Mrs. Wright told her. "Your hospitality and friendship is really appreciated."

Jonathon awoke from a restful night's sleep and began his morning walking exercises. The heavy and awkward cast made it more difficult, but he was determined to maintain the muscular integrity of his legs. He walked through the ward out toward the terrace where he could watch the river. He could also see the parking lot for the hospital below and checked to see if his mother's Nash was still in the lot. On his last trip around the circuitous route he saw Lisa stop her Studebaker next to the Nash. Faith stepped out of the back seat taking two small suitcases from the trunk and placing them in her grandmother's car. Jon smiled. His daughter was growing up. He watched them talk for a while, then, Mrs. Wright embraced Terry and Lisa. Faith kissed Terry on the cheek and warmly embraced Lisa for a long time. He sighed thinking that Hope's death must have been as traumatic for Faith as it was for him. She deserved better from her father!

Jon was disappointed when he saw Lisa's car leave the parking lot. He waved to Faith and his mother.

Lisa and Terry visited the York Beaches and sat on a rock at the Nubble Lighthouse, watching the restless sea smash relentlessly on the granite shore. They watched coast guard members pull themselves across the water that separated the lighthouse from the mainland. A strong cable was suspended between two poles. The men rode in a wooden box with a pulley that rolled along the cable overhead. Gravity pulled them over the roiling water to the landing on the lighthouse island.

Terry was fascinated by the coast guardsmen as they climbed into the tower of the lighthouse high on the ledge. He could see them working around the large lamp at the top. Lisa explained that people stay at the lighthouse all night to make sure that the light always shines. If it went out, there was a danger that passing ships would hit the rocky promontory and sink. They heard the powerful fog horn being tested by the men. It startled Terry and he clung to his mother. She smiled at his instinctive move. He needed her and that need gave meaning to her life.

They drove around the beaches for a couple of hours and spent some time at the fishing docks at York Harbor watching the boats discharge their daily catch of fish and lobsters. By two o'clock, Terry was beginning to tire, so she headed for home. She wanted to check in on Jon before returning to Durham. They found him sitting on the terrace in a wheelchair.

"I was expecting to see Faith and your mother," Lisa told him. Each time she saw him, he looked stronger.

"I'm glad you dropped in. I was disappointed when you left this morning. Mother and Faith were pleased with your hospitality. That was swell of you Lisa. Thanks."

"You're welcome," Lisa replied modestly. "Your mom is a wonderful lady. I enjoyed her company. Faith is a bright young lady. Her ear is uncannily well-tuned for music. She asked me to play for her and I saw her follow my fingers with an experienced eye. She's a lovely girl and you're a lucky dad to have her."

"She has made her dad proud," Jon agreed. "Mom has always been an angel. I guess that goes for most mothers. They were anxious to get home to Monson before dark. They left mid-afternoon. Mom's eyesight is not the best after dark."

"I wanted to ask if you read the note," Lisa inquired. "I still can't believe it, after five years…"

"I thought your reply was heartfelt and sincere. I believe the gentleman will be pleased to receive it. I've already sent it out," answered Jon, looking at Terry watching the boats on the river from the terrace rail. "He's a very well-mannered child. Is that because his mom is a schoolmarm?"

Lisa was surprised and looked into his eyes. He was teasing her! "I think it's possible," she smiled.

"You should smile more often, Lisa," Jonathon declared unexpectedly and quickly changed the subject. "Tell me, how many students are at the university now?"

"Maybe 1200," answered Lisa, blushing under his intense glances. "Over half of the student body are veterans from the war studying under the G.I. Bill. As a group they are the most dedicated students, consequently, the campus is probably more oriented toward academics than when you graduated in 1941. The vets are much more interested in learning than they are in partying or pulling adolescent pranks."

"I can believe that. What a wonderful opportunity for the vets. I'm most anxious to get back to work. This inactivity and waiting for wounds to heal are beginning to get me down. I've still got to go through therapy sessions for my right arm when the cast is removed."

"Patience is a virtue, Jon. Your wounds could have been worse," Lisa mentioned matter-of-factly.

A nurse interrupted their conversation. "Here's your coffee and a piece of apple pie you requested, Colonel. Do you want me to feed you?"

"No thanks, nurse," Jonathon answered, embarrassed about his condition. The nurse set the tray on the fold-down shelf on the wheelchair and left. The coffee cup had a long straw so that he could sip it without assistance. When no one was around he could eat some of the pie by eating it like a dog eating out of a bowl.

"I'd be glad to feed you, Jonathon," Lisa offered, sensing his discomfort. "It smells like homemade."

"So far, the food here has been great. Soon I'll be able to feed myself. Before you do that, would you mind pushing me to the rail beside Terry? There's a new sub tied up at the dock and it's a beauty."

"We're coming up to join you, Terry," Lisa pushed the chair to the rail. Terry turned to look at them and grinned.

Lisa fed Jon small pieces of apple pie. He was self-conscious and avoided making eye contact with her. She shared the fact that she was involved in the formation of a symphony orchestra at the university while she fed him. When the pie was finished Lisa asked Terry to place the empty tray on a table near the entrance to the terrace. Always glad to do errands, Terry complied.

Suddenly, a deep voice cried out, "Get that damned Jap kid out of here."

Terry dropped the tray and ran to his mother frightened at the loud outburst. He knew it was directed at him. Jonathon turned his head to see what was going on, and saw a marine sergeant sitting in a wheelchair pointing a menacing finger at Terry.

"That language won't accomplish anything, Sergeant. The war is over. If you can't control your mouth, then leave the terrace," Jonathon replied indignantly.

"Oh, so doggie man is a Jap lover..." the marine countered viciously.

Lisa whispered in Terry's ear, "You stay here beside Colonel Wright, I'll be right back."

"If I were a man, I'd make you eat those words," Lisa confronted the marine holding a Dixie paper cup of water and threw it in his face. The marine gasped and turned red with rage. Several patients on the terrace erupted with claps and whistles. Lisa returned to Jonathon and grasped Terry's hand, trembling, and on the verge of tears. A nurse that had witnessed what took place ran to the angry marine and told him that if he could not control himself around other people, they had ways of insuring that it wouldn't happen again. She wheeled the marine off the terrace.

Jonathon felt helpless that he could do nothing about the unfortunate scene. Lisa's silent tears touched him. "Please, Lisa. Don't take it to heart and don't take it personally."

"How can it be taken any other way, Jon?" Lisa snapped back.

"I apologize for the outrage," Jonathon replied. "That patient has been quite unruly since he was transferred to this hospital."

"Terry and I have got to go. I didn't mean to cause a scene."

"Will you come again?" Jonathon asked, upset that she was leaving under these circumstances.

"Do you want me to?" she inquired of him. The question conveyed all the anxieties and doubts that had been a part of her lately.

Jon saw the uncertainty in her eyes. "You and I have not shared a lot of time together, yet, I feel as if I've always known you, Lisa. I don't know how to say it, but I'd be saddened if you did not want to visit again."

Lisa wiped her tears away. "I believe with all my heart that you saved my life, Jonathon. You've been in my thoughts every day since the prison raid. If you wish, I'll be back, possibly next weekend. The week days are busy, but I'll try my best."

"Thanks old friend."

Lisa softly kissed him on the lips and left the terrace with Terry in tow.

Chapter Eighteen

For the remainder of the fall, Lisa visited Jonathon every weekend. She tried to be cheerful and upbeat, bringing him news and gossip circulating at faculty meetings and on campus. Jonathon was determined to minimize the loss of his left hand. Doctors had removed his body and arm casts early in October and told him that his body wounds were healing satisfactorily. The stub of his left arm extended to within an inch of his elbow, and had healed enough so that the Navy designed and constructed an artificial arm and hand to fit his configuration.

Jonathon's mother and Faith visited every two or three weeks and occasionally stayed with Lisa and Terry. By Thanksgiving he was strong enough to take day trips away from the hospital. He did not wear his artificial limb on the trips because what remained of his arm was not strong enough to accept it. He was still undergoing intense physical therapy to build up his shoulder and upper arm muscles so that he would be able to activate the sensitive controls being built into his mechanical arm. He stubbornly refused to wear it in public until he had mastered it completely. On those occasions when he left the hospital, he wore his uniform with an empty sleeve. He preferred that, to the embarrassment of using his new arm in public when he was not fully in control of it.

One day late in November, Lisa left Terry with a neighbor, and picked Jonathon up at the hospital. His uniform was covered with combat ribbons. The Medal of Honor was his highest award but his all-time favorite was the Combat

Infantryman Badge, a rectangular blue badge with an embossed Kentucky rifle in silver. She drove the faithful Studebaker back to the university in and around the campus. Jon had graduated in 1941, eleven years ago. Several changes had taken place since then. More buildings had been built and the lawns and sprawling campus grounds had been extended in every direction.

Lisa pulled the car to a stop beside the athletic field where ROTC units were going through drill maneuvers. Some were more proficient than others, and Jon smiled at their youthfulness and inexperience. With time, they would improve. Jon was anxious to take on the duties of commanding them. The army was holding him back, because they did not want him to be in the classroom until he was completely ready to assume the full responsibility of the post and use his new mechanical arm with ease. He was able to convince them that those requirements could keep him out of the classroom for months, and a combat veteran, he successfully argued, was fully capable of teaching and carrying out administrative duties with or without both arms. The fact that he had been grievously wounded in combat made his position as a leader and a teacher that much more valid and meaningful.

"I loved the years I spent on campus," Jon remarked. "It's encouraging to note the large number of veterans studying for degrees. I can hardly wait to become a part of the academic world."

He turned to Lisa behind the wheel of the Studebaker, finding her in a reflective mood with an allusive air of detachment. He had often thought that she could easily fit into the role of a lovable eccentric, which every institution of higher learning proudly claimed as one of their very own. At times, he saw sadness and disbelief in her eyes. She seemed to be somewhere in another world. Probably the grotesque memories from her imprisonment would never completely leave her. Other than those rare moments he was able to identify, she seemed to be happy and content with life. The past few months he had had a chance to get to know her better, but she continued to be an enigma. He had a feeling that no matter how well he knew and understood the quiet, unassuming auburn-haired lady, there would always be a part of her that was yet to be discovered. His initial admiration and respect had grown as he came to know her better.

"How about you, Lisa? Do you like teaching at the university as well as you did back home in elementary school?"

She felt his penetrating study of her. "I like it much better. It gives me more time to sharpen my own skills and I never cease to be amazed at the large pool of talent in the student body. I'm also enthused about the symphony orchestra," she acknowledged energetically.

"I read a piece in the paper about the orchestra. You must be proud of it. Are most of its members students?" Jon asked.

"Half are students and the other half faculty and local musicians. The orchestra reflects their young vibrant talents," Lisa told him. It was obvious that music was an important part of her life. Jon thought that it very well could have been the single most stabilizing element. "It should offer all the people of the community a common experience of good music, shared at the same time at the same performance. It should reflect the community where it plays and offer a variety or mix of types of music to suit everyone's taste. At Christmas time, for example, people's heartstrings resonate with the times and memories of childhood. To be part of an ensemble that is capable of evoking those kinds of feelings is wonderful and a privilege," she related happily. "I'm sorry if I carried on too much."

Jon could not keep from smiling at her sincere enthusiasm. "The University is lucky to have you, Lisa. I always knew there was something special about you."

She blushed at his compliment and looked out the window. "I've had similar thoughts about you, too. It would be impossible for me to verbalize the influence you had on me when I was on the precipice. I was ready and completely prepared to take that final plunge to oblivion until you uttered those kind words to me." She turned to face him, her eyes glistening.

He saw that detached look again and passed her a clean handkerchief. She accepted it and dabbed at her eyes. She was beautiful, mysterious, and unpredictable. Jonathon remained silent until she controlled her emotions, touched by the depth of her sensitivity. He felt privileged because she probably selected her friends very carefully, the way she had done in prison.

"I haven't thanked you enough for the kindness and generosity you've shown to my mother and daughter. Faith is a great fan of yours. It's been nice to see that kind of enthusiasm in her. She was very close to her mother. I'm afraid that I haven't been a very good dad to her."

"Did you know that she asked me to give her piano lessons when you start at the university?"

"Yes," Jon replied. "I scolded her for being too pushy."

"Oh, I'd be glad to give her lessons. She has a natural talent that should be cultivated. She's the kind of student any teacher would love to have." Lisa returned the handkerchief. "I was curious about your record at the university, so I looked it up. I didn't know you had a degree in criminology."

"It's a far cry from being an Army Ranger isn't it?" answered Jon, amused at her curiosity and candor in admitting it. "I had plans of leaving the army after the war and looking for a job with some police department."

"What made you change your mind?" she asked, instantly regretting the question. "I'm sorry, forget that I asked you that. How insensitive of me! I didn't mean to open old wounds."

"You don't need to apologize for being curious and truthful, Lisa. To be honest, staying in the army was a cowardly act for me. It was a convenient escape, an excuse to evade my responsibility to Faith as a parent. I've agonized over that decision a lot while I've been idle recovering from my injuries. I guess the good Lord knows best. I would probably have continued to deny Faith if I had not been wounded in Korea. I'm thankful for a chance to think about the things that are important in life, and I've been ashamed of my track record so far. That's when I begged the army to not discharge me until I've had a chance to do a tour of duty as a teacher. It'll be an excellent transitional position so that I can get my life in order. I don't know what I would have done without Mother."

"It sounds to me as if you've thought this thing out quite thoroughly. It must have been horrible for Faith to lose her mother at such a vulnerable age. I can't imagine Terry having to face a future without me."

"What about you, Lisa?" Jon curiously inquired. "I recall hearing Madame June say that you were engaged to get married!"

Lisa knew that at some point she would share that traumatic experience with Jon. She searched for the right words. "Jeff and I were engaged before the war. We were very much in love with each other and grew up as childhood sweethearts. The last time I saw him, just before the war ended, I was pregnant. My pregnancy and what it represented, was too much for him to handle. To make a long story short, I was given two choices, Jeff or the baby I was carrying. There were no possible exceptions. It was a simple and brutal either/or choice." Lisa watched Jon's reaction. "I chose to have the baby, and have never regretted the decision. I can honestly tell you that losing Jeff that way and the memories we shared, has been a long and painful process."

"I'm sorry, Lisa, I had no right to ask you that. Forgive me," he pleaded, meeting her deep expressive brown eyes.

"Let's not talk about the past anymore. Let's just enjoy the day. It's nice to have a chance to play hooky from the hospital."

"Would you like to go somewhere for a bite to eat?"

"Do you know of a good steak house? The hospital food isn't bad but I'd like a juicy steak, medium rare!" They smiled at each other.

"We can go to Yoken's in Portsmouth. I've never been there but my friends at school tell me it's one of the best," suggested Lisa, starting the Studebaker.

"You're the chauffeur Lisa, but this dinner is on me, I insist."

"If you insist," she replied shifting into high gear.

"Your Studebaker goes along pretty good. I have a Nash. My mother uses it to travel back and forth to the hospital. I hope I'll be able to drive soon. I'm getting cabin fever being cooped up for so long," Jon complained. "I know it's necessary, but that's not the same thing as enjoying it."

"I went to the Studebaker garage last month for grease and an oil change. While I was there, they let me try out a brand new V/8 model with an automatic transmission. There was no clutch pedal! It was a really nice car. I hated to give it back to them," she laughed. "Maybe one of those would be suitable for you."

Jon was looking out the window and responded in a defensive tone. "You mean for a one-armed man?"

"No, no I didn't mean it the way you're taking it," exclaimed Lisa. "I'm sorry. I never meant to offend you. Please..."

"I know what you meant, Lisa," he replied quickly. "I've seen the ads for the new Studebakers and thought the same thing. I didn't mean to take offense. It's just that I still haven't come to grips about having only one arm. I'm adapting to it, but to be truthful, I feel a little like a cripple that will never be whole again."

Lisa abruptly pulled the Studebaker off the road and came to a sudden stop. She turned to Jon with her bright eyes glistening. "I'm sorry I brought up the subject, Jon. You completely misread what I intended to say. I understand your concern—even your distaste about losing an arm. It's only natural. Please, whatever you do, don't be pulled into that self-pity mode. You're above that. In many ways you came out of two wars with injuries that were bad enough, but they could have been worse. Some didn't survive. You know that better than anyone. How dare you call yourself a cripple? Do Faith or your mother think of you as a cripple? Cripples don't earn the Medal of Honor ribbon you wear.

"The kind considerate soldier that came out of the jungle to free me and my companions could never be a cripple. Don't use that word in my presence. I hate it because it's synonymous with inadequacy and becomes an excuse for not measuring up. I've been down that road, and I can tell you it's a dead ender."

Jonathon was taken aback by her outburst. He saw a new Lisa. Strong passions and feelings were just below the surface! "I hear you, Lisa. I guess I had that scolding coming to me. Wow, you can really chew out a guy when he needs it."

Lisa chuckled at him and herself. "Sometimes I can get worked up. I didn't mean to bark at you."

"Do you know that when you're angry you're very beautiful?" he replied.

"You're teasing me now," she said nervously.

"No, I'm not." He tilted her chin upward with his right hand and gently kissed her on the lips. She clasped her arms around his neck and returned his kiss.

Tears formed in Lisa's eyes. They both remained silent for a long time, enjoying the moment. Then, Jonathon pulled a clean handkerchief from his pocket and carefully wiped away her tears. He kissed her trembling lips and she began to cry again. It was a powerful moment of discovery for each of them.

"I believe I've fallen in love with you, Lisa. It was easy to do you know," he whispered in her ear.

"Oh, Jonathon! I've loved you since that first day," she cried between sobs. "I wanted so much to be your friend. Every day I've spent visiting with you has been the highlight of my existence. I didn't dare to hope that my feelings would be reciprocated."

"How can a person not love you? These past weeks with you have been like a ray of sunshine in my life. I never thought any person could ever have a place in my heart, but you've won it with your gentle and positive ways. The days have been long between your visits to the hospital. When you do show up the whole place glows with your presence." Jon clasped her hand in his.

"It's almost like a song," said Lisa in a low tremulous voice. "Two lonely people finding love after bitter losses and rejection. I've had many offers at the university and back home. None have been appealing to me. Now I know why I kept refusing them. Is this for real Jonathon? I couldn't handle another rejection and that's the reason I've been reluctant to place myself in that position."

"I didn't plan this, Lisa. I've cherished our friendship. It wasn't difficult to have it take one more step forward. Lately, I've been thinking that maybe, just maybe, you would not want a one-armed man…"

"Stop right there, Colonel Wright," Lisa said sharply. "Those are your thoughts, not mine. If you only knew how much I've leaned on your strong principles. I made the decision to have Terry after talking to you on the hospital ship. You've been my salvation in more ways than you'll ever know. I can tell you with all my heart that I love you without reservations. It has been a secret dream of mine over the years."

Jon held her again and buried his face in her hair. Suddenly his world had changed. He looked into her eyes again and wiped a tear that was falling down the side of her nose and kissed her one more time. Lisa embraced him. Her heart was pounding wildly. She felt like shouting to the world that her love for Jon had at last been declared, and the joy was compounded. He loved her too!

Chapter Nineteen

It was a day that Lisa and Jonathon would always remember! Their first meal out at Yoken's was an experience they did not want to end. It had been Jon's first trip out from a hospital since he was wounded in Korea.

At first, he was self-conscious appearing in public with an empty sleeve. Lisa was able to dispel his anxiety by telling him that people may stare, but they do so because his ribbons and empty sleeve only serve to indicate that he was a brave soldier and has sacrificed much for his country. Most acknowledged him with respect, not pity.

Lisa also saw that he was getting tired. "I don't want you to overdo on your first outing. Why don't I take you back to the navy yard?" She took his right hand in hers across the table. "I never dreamed that this day would be such a happy one for me."

"I'll let you take me back. I am feeling a little tired, but it feels good. It's hard to explain."

"I understand, Jon. Where do we go from here?" she asked. "Do you want me to help you find a house or apartment near the university? Have the doctors given you any idea just when you can start your teaching tour?"

"The doctors are cautious about predictions. I expect that I'll be able to carry out a full day's work within a couple of months. I'd prefer starting earlier on a part-time basis. I'm not sure what the routine will be for quarters, Lisa. I'll find out later how the army handles that. It'll be nice working with you in the same place."

"I've been thinking the same thing," Lisa remarked casually. "I'm ready to leave if you are. We can be at the navy yard in a half hour." She noticed a distressed look on his face. "Are you all right, Jon?"

He was holding his wallet in his right hand. "I need some help," he replied embarrassed at his predicament. "Would you hold the wallet while I remove the money to pay the bill?"

"Of course. Don't feel bad. It'll be easier when they have your arm ready. In the meantime, let me be the one to help you for a change. Okay, Colonel?"

Touched by the love in her eyes, Jon replied. "Okay, Lisa Carter!"

On the way back to the hospital, Lisa was focused and alert with her driving, enjoying the closeness of Jonathon's presence. Words were not necessary for her to rejoice that, for the first time in years, she was truly happy. The future was bright with possibilities. As she was driving over the bridge between Portsmouth, New Hampshire, and Kittery, Maine, Lisa remembered that she had not told Jon about the symphony's schedule.

"I almost forgot to tell you," she continued. "Our schedule for the winter performance is beginning to come together. We're doing a Christmas concert on Christmas Eve and a couple of months or so later, we're doing a concert at the auditorium with two featured performers. One is a cello player and the other is a violinist. Commitments are tentative but it's exciting to think about."

"I'm glad for you, Lisa. I hope that I can attend them. Faith asks me every time I see her when you're going to play again." Sitting beside her in the Studebaker, Jon sensed the inherent decency and modesty that was so much a part of her disposition. He was a lucky man.

"Faith is a dear girl. You have a right to be proud of her. Your mother has done a wonderful job, but I have a feeling

174

that she is anxious to be with her dad. Just maybe, her dad needs her more than she needs him."

"You're a perceptive person. I do need her. As I mentioned earlier, I've felt guilty and hope that I can make up for lost time."

Lisa turned into the hospital parking lot and stopped. "I'm sure you will, Jon. It's been quite a day!"

"More than I expected," he answered, leaning over to kiss her.

"Thank you for being honest with me," Lisa was smiling at him. "I probably won't be able to sleep tonight. You rest well, Jonathon. I'll pray for you."

Jonathon opened the door and started to get out of the car. Lisa opened her door to get out. "Please, Lisa," he requested. "Let me get out of the car and walk back into the hospital without an escort."

She smiled at her proud soldier. "Of course. I'll see you as soon as I can make it. Probably day after tomorrow. Take care of yourself, soldier."

Jonathon climbed out of the car and walked deliberately to the door, where he turned to wave.

She watched him disappear and started the Studebaker's engine. One of the most beautiful evenings of her life was slowly fading to a memory.

Lisa's life changed dramatically that day she and Jon had declared their love. She still taught her classes in music at the university with her usual enthusiasm and maintained the same routines she had always done, but it was all accompanied now by a heightened sense of no longer being alone. Sharing her heart with Jon had made the difference. Their discovery of each other continued all that winter.

Visits to the hospital were more frequent. They often took short drives along the rocky coastline. One stormy evening they watched the crashing waves attack the granite shore in nearby York Harbor. They occasionally went to the movies. Jon attended his first film in a civilian theater in eight years. They watched *African Queen* with Humphrey Bogart and Katharine Hepburn at the Colonial Theater in Portsmouth.

Occasionally Lisa challenged Jon to a game of cribbage. She told him that Madame June had shown her how to play the game while they were in prison. In prison, the cards they had were fragile and badly worn, but they were able to use them for the duration of their incarceration. The board was usually drawn on the ground and sharpened twigs were stuck into the soft earth as pegs.

Jonathon claimed that he was considered by many in his company to be a good cribbage player. But game after game, Lisa was able to beat him. Occasionally she skunked him and that tickled her. They laughed a lot together. All of a sudden her life had taken a turn for the better and she was happy.

In the meantime, Jonathon was growing stronger with each passing day. The physical therapy section at the hospital had completed the mechanical arm and the caliper he had selected to substitute for his hand. Slowly, after days of concentrated therapy sessions, Jonathon was able to move his new arm in circles and directions that replicated movement of a real arm. At times he was discouraged with his progress, but Lisa was always there supporting his efforts and encouraging even greater participation.

The first time he appeared in public with his new arm was the Christmas concert at the university. Lisa had obtained seats for Jon, Terry, Faith, and her grandmother. She played lead piano and the primary accompaniment to the choral group performing with them. Lisa and Terry met Jon and his family at the hospital and they all went to Yoken's to celebrate the occasion. It had become a favorite dining place for Lisa and Jon. Terry and Faith especially liked the bowls of fresh shrimp Jonathon had ordered for them. It was a good place to enjoy a leisurely meal and share in warm fellowship before attending the concert.

After dinner, Lisa drove back to her apartment, where she changed into her teal green gown with white lace covering her shoulders and her throat. Jon was the first to see her as she entered the living room.

"Wow, is this the same lady?" he exclaimed approvingly, getting up from the couch. His mother handed him a box containing a violet orchid. May I have the pleasure of fastening your first orchid from me?"

"Yes," she answered modestly. "It's beautiful, Jon."

"You look lovely, Lisa," Mrs. Carter told her.

"Yes, like a star," added Faith, impressed by the fact that Lisa was going to perform on the stage.

"All of you are wonderful. Thank you. Would you believe that my stomach is a buzz with butterflies!"

Jon was proud to show off some of his newly acquired skills by removing the delicate orchid from the container and setting it on the table. He then turned to Lisa positioning the corsage high on her left shoulder while he fastened it to the gown. When he had finished, he smiled and breathed easier.

"You're beautiful, Lisa," he whispered in her ear.

"I love you, Colonel Wright," she replied lightly kissing him on the cheek. "We should get going, we don't want to be late." She kneeled in front of Terry and put her arms around him. "Are you going to be a big boy for Mommie while I play in the concert? Faith, her daddy and her grandmother will be sitting with you in the front row. You watch and I'll wave to you."

"I'll be good, Mom. You're all dressed up pretty," Terry replied, kissing his mother.

"He's going to be just fine, Mother," remarked Jon, holding out his new arm for Terry. He took it without a thought and smiled at Jon.

For the past month, Jon and Lisa had taken special pains to show him how it substituted for the hand Jon had lost in the war, and that it was nothing to be frightened about. Jonathon had even taken his shirt off to show Terry how it was attached to his shoulder and upper arm. Every day Jonathon needed someone to tighten the straps around his chest and arm. When he first began wearing the arm, Lisa was instructed by the nurses and therapist about the correct tension of the straps. She insisted that Terry become a part of that same team so that he could do it if she were absent. One day Jonathon had asked him to fasten the straps all by himself, and he did a good job. That was the beginning of a very special relationship between the two. Terry idolized Jonathon, who in turn made Terry feel important to him. Lisa beamed when she saw the two men in her life interact with each other.

The Christmas concert opened with all the old familiar favorites: *Silent Night, Joy To The World,* and others. They played excerpts from George Handel's *Messiah,* which embraces the full breadth of human experiences, hope and fulfillment, suffering and death, resurrection and redemption, a perennial favorite the world over.

Lisa's piano was positioned to the left of center stage. She waved several times to Terry sitting between Jonathon and Faith directly in front of her piano. She was her usual inspiring self. Twice during the concert, she brought the audience to new levels of involvement, sharing the passion and joy of the musical selections. At the finale of the concert, the conductor and the choral director walked to the center of the stage with her. She bowed to the audience. They rose to their feet as one and gave her a resounding endorsement.

Jonathon saw the tears that filled her eyes. He picked up Terry so that he could see his mother better.

"They like my mommie don't they," Terry said to Jonathon.

"They sure do, Terry, they sure do. How lucky you are to have a mom like her," Jonathon told him, his heart pounding. He was so proud and thankful that she was a part of his life.

Twenty minutes after the concert, Lisa was able to free herself of the fans and made her way to the Studebaker in the parking lot. Mrs. Wright and Faith were holding Terry between them in the back seat. He was sound asleep with his head on Mrs. Wright's lap.

"I'm sorry I'm so late," announced Lisa climbing behind the wheel.

"You don't have to apologize, dear girl," said Mrs. Wright. "This has been a wonderful evening. I've enjoyed it so much."

"I hope that I might be able to play like that someday," Faith told her.

"You're very generous with your praise and I appreciate it. Now, what do you and your grandmother say if I take you two to the apartment? Would you look after Terry while I take your son to the hospital?"

"Faith and I will be glad to," responded Mrs. Wright uplifted to see how things were going between Lisa and her son. "Terry's out like a light. You could tie his arms and legs into knots and he'd never know it," she laughed softly. She was a gentle lady and Lisa liked her pragmatic ways.

As soon as Lisa stopped the Studebaker, Jon stepped out of the car, picked up Terry, carried him into the house, and placed him on his bed. Faith and her grandmother quickly got him undressed and slipped him into his pajamas. He was still sound asleep. Lisa excused herself to change into something less formal than her concert gown. Shortly, she reappeared wearing a deep purple blazer and skirt.

"Now I feel more comfortable," she announced. "Are you ready, Jon?"

"You bet," he answered. "I feel terrible putting you through this trouble."

"You know it's no bother," she scolded him. "Good night Faith and Mrs. Wright. I'll be quiet when I return and we can sleep late in the morning. The first one up can put on the coffee."

Mrs. Wright warmly embraced Lisa. "Goodnight, Lisa. I want you to know how grateful I am to see Jonathon's response to therapy. Thanks for giving me back my son. I understand now why he loves you the way he does."

"Mrs. Wright," Lisa sighed. "You're going to make me cry. I'm thankful to be the object of his love. You rest well and I'll see you in the morning." Lisa turned to Faith who had been looking at her as if she were ten feet tall all evening. "Goodnight, Faith. I'm glad you liked the concert. Your time will come. Probably sooner than you think."

"I love you, Mrs. Carter," confessed Faith, kissing her on the cheek.

"I love you too, honey," Lisa replied. Happiness and contentment filled her heart.

Chapter Twenty

Two months after Christmas, 1950.

The army had approved Jonathon's release from the hospital so that he could take up residence at the house they had leased for him near the university. The doctors believed that he was strong enough to handle the teaching assignment and administrative duties associated with the post. The New Hampshire ROTC contingent was composed of two lieutenants and three sergeants, all combat veterans. Jonathon would continue his therapy with the mechanical arm, even though he had passed all the requirements for the army and the State of New Hampshire for his driving permit.

The first day on the job, he drove to the campus in a Ford army sedan issued to the ROTC unit. He met Lisa walking from her apartment to the campus and stopped to give her a lift. He was all smiles. "Is it proper protocol for a new male faculty member to give a lady faculty member a ride, or is it taboo?" He leaned across the seat to open the door for her.

"You look great, Jon. I believe work will be good for you," she squeezed his hand. "In regards to conduct on campus, all kidding aside, it might be best if we avoid hugs and kisses in public, at least for awhile. What do you think?"

"You're correct, Lisa. It would be more professional and the students don't need any more gossip material. I'm sure that many will, in time, figure out that we have something going between us. My love for you is not easy to hide."

"I love you too, Jonathon. I'm so proud of you I could bust, but let's keep it our secret. It'll be fun and kind of clandestine," she giggled softly. "You could drop me off at the administration building. By the way, there's a faculty meeting this afternoon. I expect it's to introduce you to the clan, so be prepared for a thorough inspection." She pointed to the administration building known as "T" Hall. "I'll see you this afternoon. Thanks for the ride, good luck, soldier."

Jonathon checked in at the ROTC offices to introduce himself to the staff. The secretary assigned to the unit by the University told him that Sergeant Clymer was in the conference room grading papers. Jonathon walked in on him.

"Good day, Sergeant Clymer. I'm Colonel Wright."

The sergeant came to attention when he heard Jonathon speak. "I'm sorry, I didn't hear you come in, Colonel. Welcome to the campus. I hope you like what we've been doing here."

"Please, stand easy, Sergeant. I'm simply familiarizing myself with the layout. I look forward to working with you and the others. I have much to learn, so please, if you see that I'm stepping out of line and beginning to make an ass of myself, I beg of you to confront me directly and promptly. If you do that with honest convictions, you will have earned my sincere gratitude. I don't like or tolerate 'yes' men."

Sergeant Clymer checked the ribbons Jonathon wore. "That Medal of Honor ribbon has already won my respect, sir."

Jonathon noted the Combat Infantryman Badge the Sergeant wore. "That CIB you wear, Sergeant, make us part of a select fraternity. I'll be proud to work with you."

"Do you want me to show you around, Colonel?"

"Thanks, but I'll manage," replied Jonathon. "By the way, Sergeant. I would like your advice on how we should conduct ourselves in uniform on campus, especially in basic military courtesy."

"Well, sir, I've always thought of it this way. Around campus, the students watch our every move. I think we should put our best foot forward. A reasonable amount of spit and polish in how we present ourselves never does any harm. Proper and respectful salutes between officers and enlisted men is a must. The students have a tendency to look upon us as role models and they can learn much in the way we interact. May I speak freely and unofficially, sir?"

"Please do."

"Over the past twenty years I've been in the army, I've served under some of the finest officers that ever lived. I've also served under some of the most pompous assholes that ever walked. In my opinion, campuses are no place for the latter category of officer. Another thing, sir, in front of students in or out of the classroom, I would resent it if you looked down on me as an inferior. I'm a subordinate yes, but I'm good at my job. Some officers I've served with always belittle enlisted men in order to make them look more important. Am I making myself clear, sir?"

Jonathon appraised the sturdy plain-speaking professional soldier standing in front of him and smiled. He was the embodiment of the American soldier that Jonathon had come to love and respect. "I read you loud and clear, Sergeant Clymer, and I agree with every word. I'm glad we had this conversation. The army functions as a team organization. Every part of the organization is important for the whole to work. That implies that respect comes from the top down. If you ever detect that I have violated that code of respect, I'll appreciate your bringing it to my attention. Have a good day, Sergeant."

"And you too, sir."

Jonathon left the office and continued to tour around the campus and streets close to the university. The Commons building housed the cafeteria where he stopped and went through the line selecting macaroni and cheese, a fruit cup, and a glass of milk. Surveying the dining area for an empty table, he took one near the windows overlooking a terrace facing south. It gave him an opportunity to observe the flow of students, staff, and faculty as they entered and left the cafeteria. He was impressed with the maturity of the seasoned veterans going to school under the G.I. Bill of Rights. They displayed an intensity of purpose that was visibly lacking in the younger non-veteran student body. He had to admit that the horrors of combat matured a person beyond their years.

Two women about Jonathon's age scanned the dining hall for a seat and spotted him sitting alone. They approached the table and casually asked if he would mind sharing the table with them.

"Please, sit down," Jonathon said, standing to greet them. "I'm Colonel Wright, the new ROTC commander. This is my first day on the job."

"I'm Alice Raney. I teach English literature. This is Grace Mellon our language specialist."

"I'm glad to meet you." The two ladies were studies in contrast. Miss Mellon had black hair and was slightly overweight. She smiled a lot and seemed content to let the more outspoken Alice Raney dominate the conversation. Alice Raney was tall, slender and showy with blonde hair and a confident air. There was a boldness about her that made Jonathon uncomfortable.

"How nice it is that we had a chance to meet, Colonel," Miss Raney said, eyeing his ribbons. She wore a lot of makeup and looked as if she belonged on a stage with models instead of a classroom filled with students. "Is the rumor true going around the campus that you're a Medal of Honor winner?"

"I don't know where the rumor came from," Jonathon replied, eating his meal. "To answer your question, Miss Raney, yes, I do wear the Medal of Honor for action in Manila, but I wear it as a symbol for those who sacrificed and suffered and were never honored."

Miss Mellon noted his CIB. "My brother earned one of those badges with the long Kentucky rifle. He was more proud of that than of any other ribbon or medal."

"Your brother thinks the same as I, Miss Mellon." Jonathon finished his lunch and excused himself. "It's been nice meeting you two. I understand there's a faculty meeting this afternoon, maybe I'll see you there."

"Yes, we'll be there," said Miss Raney.

Miss Mellon continued to smile at him. "It's good that the army has filled the post that's been open for so long."

Jonathon chuckled to himself as he left the cafeteria. A poster on a bulletin next to the entrance caught his eye:

Annual Spring Concert

The New Hampshire Symphony Orchestra

March 15, 1951

Featuring The Internationally Acclaimed Violinist From Japan

Horio Taniguchi

He read the poster and smiled, thinking how modest it was of Lisa to not be listed. The featured performer Horio Taniguchi, quickened his pulse and started him asking questions to himself. Did Taniguchi know about Lisa? Thinking back to his visit with Taniguchi, he was certain that he never declared her name, and the letter she had asked him to send was signed "Madame X." Was it a coincidence? He was unsure! Lisa had mentioned the concert to him several times and even became excited about the chance to have a famous violinist visit New Hampshire. Little did he dream that it could be Mister Taniguchi!

Should he alert Lisa? His first instinct was that she had a right to know. If he was to tell her before the performance, it might have an adverse affect on her ability to perform and that would have been awkward to explain to the rest of the musicians in the orchestra. He had mailed Lisa's letter to Taniguchi and so far, there was no follow-up correspondence. He rode around the area for a long time troubled by the knowledge he had kept from Lisa.

Checking his watch, Jonathon drove to the building where the faculty meeting was scheduled to take place. He had prepared a short speech to deliver in case he was asked to make a statement. He had planned to review it that afternoon, but his head and heart were too busily focused elsewhere.

Most of the faculty were in the auditorium. He walked down the center of the aisle to the front row of seats where the president of the university had requested that he position himself. He scanned the seats on both sides trying to locate where Lisa was sitting, but did not see her.

The president made a few remarks to the gathered audience pertaining to some changes in the curriculum and about summer school itineraries. Then he announced two appointments to the faculty; a forestry professor named Doctor Bert Hunt, and Army Colonel Jonathon Wright. "It gives me great pleasure to announce that the university is graced by the presence of an army officer who has been awarded the Medal of Honor. Ladies and gentlemen, how about a warm welcome to Colonel Jonathon Wright." The President waved his arm towards Jonathon and the audience rose as one to welcome him.

Jonathon walked to the podium to shake hands with the president and the dean of the College of Liberal Arts. Using that opportunity to locate Lisa, he saw her in the back row directly in front of the podium. Raising both arms to the audience, Jonathon wanted them to see the mechanical arm and pair of tongs, so that they would know who and what he was. Several members of the faculty were surprised that such an injured man was allowed to continue in the Army.

"Mr. President, deans of the different colleges, faculty, and staff members. Your warm welcome is appreciated. I'm humbled to become a part of the faculty of the University I graduated from in 1941. This is my first post at an institution of higher learning. The main job of a soldier is to defend our nation against all enemies and to teach others, the young men and women, who shoulder that burden with their blood. I'm open to any suggestions or criticisms you may have about what I do in the classroom and how my performance might be improved or altered. Constructive criticism of ideas, tactics, doctrine, etc. is one of the ways our army improves its performance, so don't be afraid to speak up. Change is a constant process with soldiers. After I graduated from the university in 1941, I went to the Pacific theater of operations where I stayed for the duration of the war. I was wounded again in Korea eight months ago. I already feel that I've come home for good. Thank you for allowing me to become a part of the faculty as a soldier."

The forestry professor made a few remarks after Jonathon sat down and the President reclaimed the podium. "Before we adjourn this get-together, I want to inform you about a very special occasion that is coming up. You've probably already seen the posters around campus about our recently established New Hampshire Symphony Orchestra concert. I've been impressed by the hard work of our very own Miss Lisa Carter, who has been deeply involved in making it all possible. Stand up Miss Carter wherever you are." Lisa stood up and waved her hand. "I just wanted to say thank you on behalf of the university and the people of the state for your fine work. It is enriching the lives of each and every one of us. Thank you."

Minutes later, Jonathon was inundated by people wishing him well in his new post. They were sincere and heartfelt. It was comforting to be so warmly received. Slowly, he was able to make some headway to the back of the auditorium to Lisa. She was all smiles and extended her hand to shake with him. "You've made a successful beginning, Colonel." She squeezed his hand. He returned the pressure and grinned.

The auditorium was almost empty except for Alice Raney, who was waiting for a chance to speak to Jonathon. "So you're an alumnus, Colonel, we meet again." she said boldly.

Lisa knew the English instructor and noted her attempt at familiarity with Jonathon. At first it amused her until she heard the coy and provocative Miss Raney invite him to her place for dinner some evening at his convenience.

Jonathon was unprepared for such an invitation and had no intention of starting his debut at the college accepting invitations from strangers. "Thank you, Miss Raney. For now, I've got my hands full with my new quarters and my daughter. I'm also committed to therapy sessions each week, so I'll have little time for socializing, but thanks for asking."

Miss Raney picked up on the list of excuses and left feeling disappointed. Lisa heard the exchange between them and walked silently to the parking lot with him. "You handled that situation beautifully. She has a reputation around the campus, so tread softly, if you know what I mean."

"I know what you mean," Jonathon laughed. "How are we going to handle this? We can't pretend to be strangers and never talk to each other. I suggest that we be natural with each other and be discreet at public appearances."

"I agree. It's childish to hide what I don't want to hide," she said. "I was so proud of you, Jonathon."

"Now you know how proud I am of a certain lady when I see posters all over the campus about a concert next month."

"I meant to tell you about that. We're all so excited about the violinist that's scheduled to appear. One of the musicians in the orchestra had played years ago with this Mister Taniguchi, and had nice things to say about him. The agency that's handling his bookings has already given us a repertoire that he'll perform. I'm familiar with the selections. It should be a time to forget the war." Lisa looked at Jonathon and saw a troubled look on his face. "What's wrong, Jon?"

"Nothing, I was just thinking how wonderful it is to see your enthusiasm for a Japanese musician. I'd say that you've grown a lot, Lisa Carter. Do you know how much I love you?"

"You're going to make me cry right here in front of everybody," Lisa whispered. "Come to the house for supper tonight if you want."

"Thanks for the invite. Just think I've been on campus for only one day and I've already gotten two invitations for dinner." Jon laughed and continued, "Seriously though, I won't be able to make it for dinner. Instead could I bum a ride to Portsmouth tonight? My mother and Faith are meeting me at Warren's restaurant in Kittery. You and Terry could join us. Faith has a week off from school and wants to spend it with me in Durham. I'm thrilled about that."

"You mean you need a ride to Kittery," Lisa asked teasingly.

"Yes, but I refuse to beg," he grinned. "I've got a surprise to show you tonight."

"Can Terry come?"

"Of course," he answered, stepping close to her. "If you don't stop bugging me, I'm going to give you a hug and kiss right here."

"In that case, I'll cancel supper and meet you at your house at five-thirty. Is that all right?"

"That'll be fine, beautiful, I love you," announced Jonathon in a whisper and walked confidently away from her.

Lisa watched him with a happy heart. How nice it was to have someone to share her life with. "I love you, Colonel Wright, more than you think," she whispered to herself and continued on her way.

Chapter Twenty-One

Lisa pulled into Jonathon's driveway at five-thirty on the button. He was waiting on the porch for them and climbed into the front seat with Terry between them.

"What's your surprise?" she asked on the way to Kittery.

"I can't tell you until later in the evening after Mother leaves," Jon answered with a smirk on his face.

Faith and Mrs. Wright were waiting in the parking lot at Warren's restaurant. Lisa enjoyed seeing Faith and Jon interact. They were bonding more and more with each other and their joy was obvious. They went into the restaurant, ordered lobsters and shrimp, and sat back to relax and enjoy the evening.

Jonathon was sitting beside his mother and leaned over to whisper something in her ear. She smiled at him. "That's so nice. I'm glad for you Jon, you should reward yourself more. I'll be fine on the way back home. Don't worry about me. The Nash is running great. Faith has been looking forward to this vacation for a long time. The two of you need to be together more."

Lisa watched the exchange between mother and son and was reminded of the concern a mother always has for her child, regardless of age.

An hour and a half later, Jonathon checked his watch and announced that they had to be going. They said good-byes to Mrs. Wright and watched her leave the parking lot and head north. Jonathon asked Lisa to drive through the main street in Portsmouth on their way to Durham. After they left the heart of the city proper, he asked Lisa to turn into the Studebaker dealer's lot.

Jonathon was all excited. "The surprise I have is that I have ordered a brand new Studebaker Landcruiser sedan with an automatic transmission and their new V/8 engine."

"My, this is a surprise. I'm so glad for you," she said getting out of the car. "Is that it?" she pointed to a shiny new black cherry sedan with a windshield visor.

"It sure is. I was hoping that I could pick it up without you knowing and really surprise you," exclaimed Jon. "It's my first new car and I've had this model in mind ever since you mentioned it to me, Lisa."

They walked into the showroom and looked at several models on display while Jonathon completed signing the paperwork. He came out of the salesman's office dangling the keys in his hand, smiling from ear to ear. They went outside to his new vehicle. Faith and Terry opened all four doors to look it over. The coachwork was beautiful. The wine colored seats were soft and roomy. It smelled fresh and clean inside.

"Why don't I take Faith and Terry with me and you can follow behind us?" suggested Jonathon. "I'll be driving a little slower for a while until it's broken in."

"I can do that. It's a beauty, Jon. I agree with your mom, you deserve it and more," Lisa exclaimed, placing an arm around him.

"The army sedan is strictly for official travel, so I needed a car for personal use. I'm glad you like it. Now I can take my best girl out on a date," he whispered, lightly kissing her on the top of the head. "Okay gang let's mount up and head for home!" Terry and Faith climbed into the front seat of the Studebaker "bulletnose."

Jonathon sat behind the wheel, adjusted the seat and rear view mirrors to suit him, and touched the starter button on the dash. The powerful V/8 engine ran smooth and quiet. A feeling of contentment and pride came over him as he placed the shift selector in "D" and drove his new car out of the dealer's lot onto the street.

Later that night, after Jonathon had shown Faith around their new house and she had fallen asleep in her new bedroom, he thumbed through his bundle of mail. It was his first mail delivery at the new address. One letter with a Japanese postmark grabbed his attention. It was from Horio Taniguchi. The letter had been to a dozen or so different addresses and was dated six weeks ago! Jonathon sat at the kitchen table and read:

Tokyo, Japan

December 20, 1950

Dear Colonel Wright,

I'm sending this letter to your old address in Tokyo. I know that you are no longer there but am hoping that it will eventually find its way to you. My purpose in writing is to inform you that I've been approached by a booking agency to do up to nine concerts in the United States. My itinerary is enclosed.

It has been my fond hope that you may be able to meet me somewhere at one of my concert performances. I'm starting in Boston and New York. What I am really hoping, Colonel, is that you will be able to supply me with the name and address of the lady who answered my previous letter. When I read her reply I had a warm feeling inside and it has been years since this old man has been so profoundly touched.

I pray that this finds you in good health and empowered to grant my request. Thank you for your concern.

Respectfully yours,

Horio Taniguchi

All that night Jonathon tossed and turned, wondering what he should do. He felt in his heart that Mister Taniguchi's request was honorable and that it might ease some of the pain that he had carried for years. Just how it would affect Lisa was unpredictable. He could imagine an introduction going either badly or extremely well, granting some element of closure for her. By the time the sun spilled into his bedroom, he had made up his mind. If he was going to be the instrument of their discovery of each other, it would have to take place after the concert. He would have to time the meeting when it would be "right." Beyond that, he had no way of protecting Lisa from being hurt, and that very real possibility bothered him.

Jonathon was relieved when the day of the concert arrived. It was a warm sunny day for March. Some of the winter's supply of snow had already melted. He had volunteered to take Faith and Terry with him to his house for the day while Lisa prepared for the concert and met with the musicians for last minute changes and adjustments. Terry enjoyed being with Jonathon. He was especially attracted to Faith who was patient and paid a lot of attention to him.

Lisa had a long discussion with the conductor of the orchestra, who told her that Mr. Taniguchi had requested a meeting with her, at least for an hour, in the auditorium and with the same piano that she would play at the concert. Lisa thought that sounded like a good idea and promised to be there early for the meeting. Then, she went home to bathe and dress for the occasion. She was a bundle of nerves and took a long relaxing bath before getting dressed.

Lisa had played as an accompanist with several singers and cello players, but very few violinists. She knew from experience that some musicians could be very difficult to work with because they had inflated egos. She was always aware that they were the main attraction, not her, and her job was to help them make their performance better. It could be a difficult juggling act, but over the years Lisa had handled the job with grace and professionalism. If the two did not get along, there were numerous opportunities to make either player look bad.

Lisa worried if she was good enough for the internationally acclaimed Taniguchi, and she was nervous about their meeting. Lisa's signature dress was her teal gown with white lace circling her neck and throat. For this particular concert, she had let her hair grow long so that it fell loose about her shoulders. She pinned the fresh orchid from Jonathon on her gown and checked her watch. The concert began at 7:00 PM with the doors opening at 6:00. She wanted to be at the auditorium at least by 4:30, so she gathered her purse and cape and left the house.

Theaters and auditoriums were lonely places when the lights were dimmed and the seats were empty. Lisa entered through the stage entrance, flipped on the main stage lights, and made her way to the piano. The overhead lights made her auburn hair sparkle. The pearl necklace and diamond earrings she wore were a parting gift from the director of the Boston Pops Orchestra. They too glittered as she moved across the stage, sat at the piano, and ran through some of the evening's selections.

Unbeknownst to Lisa, a small figure of a man was sitting in the front seat of the auditorium. He had been sitting in the dark trying to get a feel for the people who would be in the audience. He watched Lisa come onto the stage and sit at the piano. She was younger than he expected. He quickly approached her.

Lisa saw him climbing the side steps to the stage. She rose and turned to him. "I'm Lisa Carter. You must be Mister Taniguchi."

"Yes, I'm Horio Taniguchi," he proclaimed in English, bowing to her. "It's gracious of you to meet me."

"I'm thrilled to have an opportunity to accompany you, sir. I hope that you are satisfied with my playing. I'll do everything in my power to assist you in the performance. We're honored to have you come so far so that we can enjoy your music."

"I'm pleased to hear that, Miss Carter. I agreed to do this tour because I believe it is time to heal old wounds of war. The battered world needs the soothing benefits of music, for it has a universal message all peoples understand. I'd like to think that my tour will help to build bridges that the terrible war has torn apart."

"That's a noble undertaking, Mr. Taniguchi. I support your efforts," Lisa said, surprised at how comfortable and at ease she felt in his presence. "Our symphony orchestra is composed of a wide range of musicians. Many are still students at the university. What they lack in experience or professional skills, they make up with their passion and love of music."

"Ah, who could ask for more!" he exclaimed with a smile.

"Our program tonight is heavy to Beethoven," Lisa told him. "The orchestra is doing portions of his sixth and ninth symphonies. I love Beethoven. His compositions that describe a pastoral country life are wonderful. He had the genius of filling his music with human emotions. They're my favorites."

"I see that we have that in common, Lisa. May I call you that? You may call me Mister T if you like. I understand that New Englanders have lazy tongues." Mister T smiled with her and began taking his violin out of its case.

"Please, call me Lisa, Mister T," she said happily. She had a premonition that this was going to be a very special night!

He removed his violin from the case and gently plucked the strings. He adjusted two of them and ran his nimble fingers up and down the scale drawing the bow once across the strings in a slow steady movement. "Do you mind if we try portions of Beethoven's Sixth?"

"Whatever you request, Mister T. What a beautiful instrument," Lisa acknowledged. "Is it a Stradivarius?"

"You have keen eyes, Lisa. Yes, it's an original Stradivarius. The tone is superb. It was a gift from a beautiful Italian violinist who had to stop playing because of rheumatism in his hands. Every time I play I do so in his memory."

"I think you are a very kind man, Mister T. I'm ready when you are," she announced. Lisa was never a nervous player. She had that rare quality of being able to relax and focus on the music the minute she started to play.

She normally had a soft touch on the keys, but when she accompanied a soloist, her touch became even softer so as to not compete with the soloist. For ten to fifteen minutes, Lisa and Mr. T went through several pages of music. She had the gift of being able to fill in the breaks between notes so that the soloist's style sounded richer and more vibrant. Several times Mister T intentionally deviated from the tempo and beat of the score just to check on Lisa's response. He nodded his head in approval when she followed him instantly as if she were reading his mind. It was almost as if they were playing as one!

When they finished the passage, Mister T laid his instrument on the piano and applauded her. "Bravo Lisa bravo. You play with your heart. I'm going to enjoy this performance tonight," he exclaimed enthusiastically.

"Thank you," she replied modestly.

"I have a suggestion, Lisa," said Mister T. "I'll depend on your opinion, so be honest with me."

"I promise to be honest with you."

"Would it be appropriate, since we have a relatively youthful audience, to do an encore on a lighter note, with some of the more enduring popular songs?"

"I think the audience will love it. The orchestra is capable of handling a wide variety of songs, even country music."

"Some of your American country music is poignant and beautiful in its simplicity," noted Mister T. "I might even do an old fashioned hoe-down for a grand finale."

Lisa was drawn to his sincerity and humanity. In the few minutes they had been together she had the privilege of seeing the human side of the man and realized that it was the secret of his success as a master musician. He was a genius at his craft and he had fun doing it!

Jonathon finished putting on his necktie and checked the clock on his bedroom bureau. "Faith," he hollered out the door. "We should be leaving in a few minutes."

"I'll be ready, Daddy," she answered.

When Jonathon came out of the bedroom into the living room, he saw Terry sitting quietly on the couch looking at a comic book. "How are you doing, Terry?" Jon kneeled down in front of him. "This is going to be an exciting evening for all of us, especially your mom. Before we go to the auditorium do you want something to eat or drink?"

"I'm still full with the sandwiches Faith fixed for us," he replied. He was a serious little boy. Over the past few months, Jonathon had become attached to the child. He had good manners, which was a reflection of growing up with his mother and he listened well when he was asked to do something. He and Faith got along well. She was the big sister he never had.

"I'm all set," announced Faith, entering the room and doing a twirl in the center of the floor to show off her new teal dress.

"You and Lisa are dressed in the same colors," Jonathon noted. "I guess we can get going now. Are you anxious, Faith?"

"Oh, Daddy. You can't know how much I've looked forward to this concert. Lisa has talked a lot about the orchestra to me. When I go to school I'm going to play in one too."

"That would be nice, honey. You look lovely tonight. I'm glad we're going to have some time together. I love you." Jonathon hugged his daughter and kissed her on the top of her head.

"I love you too, Daddy, and I'm awfully proud of you. You look handsome in your uniform."

"Flattery will get you anything," he laughed, grabbing the car keys from the counter. "Lets mount up and move out." Terry followed Faith out the door.

The auditorium was beginning to fill. Jonathon parked the car in the parking lot and locked it. He held his arms out for the children to hang on to him. Faith held his right hand and Terry grasped the tong on his artificial arm. He was as comfortable with it as he would have been with his right hand. They had reserved seats in the front row near the piano. The stage curtain had been removed for the orchestra, because it used up all of the main stage area plus the front extension. Lisa's piano was always to the left of the conductor's platform and positioned so that she could see the conductor when he was at the podium. Soloists and singers had a position marked on the stage floor where they stood so that, at a glance, she could watch the conductor and the soloist at the same time without moving her head from the music rack on the piano.

Jonathon sat Terry between Faith and himself. He leaned over to ask Terry if he had to use the bathroom. Terry shook his head, slightly embarrassed. Jonathon squeezed his little hand and Terry squeezed it back. It was a simple gesture but it filled Jonathon with contentment. He recalled reading somewhere that to be loved by a small child was the ultimate compliment. He was inclined to believe that it was true.

The lights in the auditorium blinked twice and dimmed. The stage flood lights were amplified as the orchestra members filed across the stage to take their assigned positions.

They saw Lisa walk directly to the piano. She bowed to the audience and took her seat. She was beautiful and Jonathon felt his heart beat faster. The conductor was the last to come on stage. He was a relatively young man. Jonathon recognized him as one of the senior ROTC members. He bowed to the orchestra and turned to bow to the audience.

"Ladies and gentlemen," he announced. "Thank you for coming to the New Hampshire Symphony Orchestra winter concert. Tonight we have a variety of selections for your enjoyment. At the heart of our presentation will be passages from Beethoven's Sixth and Ninth Symphonies, which describe a pastoral setting not unlike our own New Hampshire countryside. We are thrilled to also include different types of music to reflect the different tastes of our community. Now, sit back, relax, and enjoy our interpretations."

The orchestra began with opening passages from Beethoven's Sixth Symphony. The classical passages held the audience spellbound. The transition from classical to contemporary selections was seamless and the audience followed closely those portions from Broadway musicals, such as *Guys and Dolls* and *The King and I*. For an hour the orchestra played without a break, doing Scottish and Irish folk songs and a large number of currently popular selections including, *Goodnight Irene, Mona Lisa,* and *Buttons and Bows*.

The conductor then turned to the audience. "Tonight we are honored to present to you an internationally famous violinist from Japan. It is a privilege and my distinct pleasure to introduce Mister Horio Taniguchi." The conductor held out his left hand to a short white-haired man in a black tuxedo and bow-tie. Mister Taniguchi bowed to the conductor and to the audience. The conductor shook his hand and directed him to the microphone. The audience gave him a warm welcome.

Mister Taniguchi stood in front of the microphone holding his violin and bow in his left hand. He raised his right hand in acknowledgment of the reception. He was a very dignified looking figure. The audience slowly became quiet. Mister Taniguchi bowed again to the audience and talked into the microphone. "Thank you, thank you for receiving this humble fiddle player with such enthusiasm. I was anxious to come to America before I became too old to play. I want to bring the soothing power of music to our war-torn world, one more time. Music touches everyone's heart and what a privilege it is for me to carry that message to people like you. Well," he smiled and scanned the audience side to side, front to back. "I came here to play the fiddle not to lecture. I'm sure you're familiar with the lovely lady who will accompany me tonight—Miss Lisa Carter." He motioned her to take a bow.

Lisa curtsied to the audience and to Mister Taniguchi and sat down. Mister T left the microphone and took his position marked on the floor near Lisa's piano. He caught Lisa's eye and paused for a second then began his rendition of one of Beethoven's most moving pieces of music—the Ninth Symphony.

Jonathon couldn't take his eyes off Lisa and Mister Taniguchi. The two musicians were completely synchronized and became as one with the music. Their interpretation of the emotions expressed by the composer were felt by the audience as well as the performers.

Mister Taniguchi played the violin with long sweeps of the bow across the strings, creating a smooth continuity to the melody without a break between the notes. He held the notes for a long time pulsated with a frequency that embraced the full spectrum of human experiences. It was the work of a gifted master. Exquisite sounds filled the auditorium, elevating the musical experience to new heights. The music embraced both performers as well as the audience—part of the magic he imparted to every composition he played.

Lisa radiated with happiness. The music had touched her in a way it had never done before. It was almost as if she were playing and hearing the selections for the very first time. Tears of rapture filled her eyes. When the composition ended quickly and with a flurry, the audience was so enthralled that it took a few seconds for them to respond. And they did so with a standing ovation that rattled the auditorium walls.

Mister T's eyes were also glistening. He looked at Lisa and motioned for her to take a bow. She did so and the applause continued for a long time. When it ended, Mister T's eyes again met Lisa's and they began an encore of popular songs including *Canadian Sunset, Shrimp Boats, Cry*, and *Ghost Riders In The Sky*.

The Japanese fiddle player, as he called himself, captivated the audience. Again and again he was called back, for five encores. The applause was spontaneous and enthusiastic. He did a few Broadway musical numbers and more contemporary music. He held up his hand in salute after the fifth encore then started a bouncing rendition of *Turkey In The Straw*, a traditional hoedown. It brought the crowd to its feet again. Tears streamed down Mister Taniguchi's cheeks as he played the final notes.

Lisa was entranced. Never had she experienced such profound emotions from music. She bowed to the audience and to Mister T. He placed his violin on the piano and embraced her. Their tears joined as one.

Jonathon absorbed the power of the performance and the response from the audience, and wondered if he had made a mistake in not telling Lisa who Mister T really was. Terry and Faith were also caught up in the energy that filled the auditorium. The orchestra left the stage for a short intermission. Jonathon was unable to contain his misgivings. He grabbed Terry and Faith and climbed the side steps to the stage where he confronted Lisa and Mister T. Still holding Terry in his left arm, Jonathon embraced Lisa. She wrapped her arms around the two of them.

"Lisa," he cried.

She saw the desperation in his eyes. "What's wrong, Jonathon?"

"I have to tell you that Mister Taniguchi is Terry's grandfather." He was filled with emotion, but he had carefully sounded each word so that she would not misunderstand him.

She looked in his eyes with disbelief. "Are you sure, Jon?"

"Yes."

"I knew there was something special about him," she answered, dazed by the revelation, yet, not surprised. The music had bonded the two! She released Jonathon and Terry.

"Do you want me to tell him?" asked Jonathon breathlessly.

"No, I will do that," she answered, taking Terry in her arms. She turned to face the emotional Mister Taniguchi.

He looked deep into her eyes and at Terry. Instantly he knew without having to be told.

"Is it true? Are you the one I wrote to? Is this your son?" The elderly fiddle player was overcome. He recognized Jonathon, and knew that his instincts were correct.

"Yes, I'm the one you wrote to. This is my son, Terry."

"I'm sorry, I feel weak all of a sudden," pleaded the passionate Mister T.

"Please, sit at my bench," suggested Lisa, helping him. "This is just as much of a shock to me as it is to you. Jonathon just told me who you are. I had no idea this would happen to Terry and me."

"May I hold Terry?" requested Mr. Taniguchi in a low voice.

Terry studied his face for several seconds. When Mister Taniguchi took one of his small hands in his, Terry was not sure just what was going on, but instinctively knew that this man who had eyes like his was a friend. Mister Taniguchi held Terry tightly, closing his eyes against the flood of tears the evening had produced. Now he knew why it was so important for him to make this tour!

203

"Tonight, in a far land, I have found fulfillment and peace for the first time in years," Mister Taniguchi told them, his face contorted with emotion. "For that I thank you, Colonel, and you Lisa. Can you forgive me?"

"Hush, Mister T," demanded Lisa, embracing him. "The past has already been buried. Let's lift our hearts and look to the future. I'd like to include you in our family circle."

"Lisa," interrupted the conductor. "Are you all right? You were magnificent tonight. The orchestra is coming in from intermission."

"I'll be fine thanks," she replied, taking Terry from his grandfather and passing him to Jonathon. "Thank you for making this possible. I love you so much."

Jonathon took Terry from his mother. "Lisa, will you marry me?"

"Yes, oh my… yes! I hope tonight never ends."

And life becomes an endless song…

Chapter Twenty-Two

Postscript

On May 18, 1972, Second Lieutenant Terry Carter Wright, United States Army, graduated third in his class from the United States Military Academy at West Point, New York.

Those who attended his graduation ceremony included the following:

His Mother, Lisa Carter Wright.

His paternal father and role model, Colonel Jonathon Wright, USA (Ret.).

His sister and best friend, Dr. Faith Wright Collins, MD.

His sister's husband, Dr. Alfred Collins, MD.

His grandfather and benefactor, Mr. Horio Taniguchi, world acclaimed violinist.

The Song Lives On!

Other Historical Novels

By

Clifton LaBree

Fading Shadows

Fading Shadows is the saga of Glenn Hastings, a severely wounded Medal of Honor recipient in World War II, and his long, tortuous search for fulfillment and happiness.......

Lake of Three Sorrows

A warm spiritually uplifting story of courage, commitment, and sacrifice. This is the story of Dale Cooper, a battle-weary American soldier who served in two world wars...

Flickering Flame *(Colonial Series Book One)*

A historical novel, about the Cullen family who settled in Portsmouth, New Hampshire, and their participation in events prior to the French and Indian War. Freedom and opportunity were on the march, but it extracted a heavy price. Frontier settlers were ruthlessly killed and butchered by rampaging Indians lead by French officers and Jesuit priests who frequently incited them to greater levels of inhumanity. A peaceful future was in jeopardy and fear gripped the land. A story of love, family and heroism on the colonial frontier.

Raising the Torch *(Colonial Series Book Two)*

A continuation of the saga from Flickering Flame, Colonial Series book one, of the Cullen family in Colonial Portsmouth, New Hampshire. This is a moving story of love and sacrifice when a small colony had the audacity to fight for independence from their motherland...

NON-Fiction Books

By

Clifton LaBree

NEW HAMPSHIRE'S GENERAL JOHN STARK, LIVE FREE OR DIE: DEATH IS NOT THE GREATEST OF EVILS

A fresh look at one of America's staunchest defenders of liberty and freedom. John Stark was a courageous New Hampshire citizen-soldier who fought in both, the French and Indian War, and the Revolutionary War. His pursuit of leadership excellence on the battlefield distinguished him as one of the most successful combat commanders of the war, and one of the least appreciated.

His selflessness, modest life style, and devotion to the cause of freedom are an inspiration that time has not diminished. He remains today the embodiment of the frugal, independent, and cantankerous New Hampshire Yankee.

GENTLE WARRIOR, GENERAL OLIVER PRINCE SMITH, USMC.

Kent State University Press. Kent, Ohio, 2001

The Story of one of the United States Marine Corps best General Officers. His flawless performance in Korea is a story that needed to be told.